*Dedicated to all those who love
nature and adventure – and suspect
there's more to this world
than meets the eye.*

Orla and the Magpie's Kiss

C. J. HASLAM

WALKER
BOOKS

With thanks to Special Agent Kate Shaw, who came on location to check the magic was real; my editor, Frances Taffinder, who made it real; to Val Thomas, whose book *Of Chalk and Flint: A Way of Norfolk Magic* confirms it's real; to my research assistant Dave T. Dog, who's also real; and to the three wise women Mrs A, Ms W and Mrs H, who will turn me into a badger if I ever reveal their names. For real.

First published 2022 by Walker Books Ltd,
87 Vauxhall Walk, London SE11 5HJ

2 4 6 8 10 9 7 5 3 1

Text © 2022 Chris Haslam
Illustrations © 2022 Paddy Donnelly

This book has been typeset in Sabon, Castellar, Cooper Black, Framboisier, Franklin Gothic, Lao MN and Marion

Printed and bound by CPI Group (UK) Ltd, Croydon CR0 4YY

British Library Cataloguing in Publication Data:
a catalogue record for this book is available from the British Library

ISBN 978-1-4063-9930-1

www.walker.co.uk

MIX
Paper from
responsible sources
FSC® C171272

CHAPTER 1

"Why all the secrecy?" muttered Richard. He gave the Manila envelope in Orla's hands an irritated glance then looked out of the window.

The 16.33 to King's Lynn was speeding through the industrial estates and Victorian terraces of north London: a damp, grey landscape of litter and advertising hoardings promising a better future. Shiny phones, greasy burgers and electric cars. Richard was admiring his reflection, oblivious.

At last he shook his head in exasperation. "We're being sent to Norfolk. Not Moscow."

Orla held up the envelope. *DO NOT OPEN BEFORE 5 P.M.* was written across the front.

"We've waited a week, so we can hang on for a few more minutes," she reasoned.

Tom came down the aisle, hand over hand on the seats to keep himself upright. He was ten – eleven in July – and delighted to be on a train without a responsible adult telling him to sit down and behave.

"Ticket collector's coming," he announced, sliding in next to Richard. He looked at Dave the dog: an eight-year-old Jack Russell terrier with legs even shorter than his temper. "That means you have to get off the seat, Dave."

Dave gave an exasperated snort and jumped onto the floor. The stick Orla carried everywhere was leaning against the carriage wall and he could see bubblegum stuck to the bottom of the table.

"We're not being sent to Norfolk," argued Orla.

"Yes, we are," said Tom.

"We had a choice," she insisted, sweeping her curly red hair from her face. "We could have gone to Gran's for the Easter holidays."

"Could we?" gasped Tom. "No one told me."

Richard scowled at Orla. "Could we?"

Orla made the face she always made when an awkward explanation was needed. "Er, it was a couple of weeks ago when Mum and I talked about it. She said it would be good to get out of the city. You were at Cubs, Tom." She glanced at Richard. "Can't remember where you were."

"How old are you?" asked Richard with a sigh.

"Thirteen."

"Exactly," said Richard. "I'm sixteen, so I should have been consulted."

"But you weren't there," said Orla reasonably.

8

Tom shook his head. "I can't believe we missed the chance to stay at Gran's."

"Norfolk will be more fun."

"No, it will not," argued Richard. "Gran would have taken us shopping."

That was true. Gran would have paid for trainers and console games and phone accessories and argued with Mum about it later.

"We'd have been surrounded by riches and died of boredom," insisted Orla. "Is it five o'clock yet?"

Richard held up his phone: 5:00:49. "Just open it and get it over with," he muttered, gazing dejectedly out of the window again as a sign saying *GasFrac: Energy as if by Magic* slid past. *Believe in the Power of Dreams* said another.

"I'm dreaming of going shopping with Gran's credit card," mumbled Richard as Orla slid a finger under the flap of the envelope and tore it straight across the top.

"Boring," she said. "You can't say that about Uncle Valentine."

Richard's expression was somewhere between dejection and depression. He looked like a prisoner en route to a Siberian gulag. "Uncle Valentine is a complete nutter," he grumbled. "His house is actually called Psycho's Creek. I don't know what Mum was thinking."

"Sicow's Creek," corrected Orla. "It's Old English for sea cows."

"Tickets, please," a guard interrupted. She was wearing a badge that said *Greater Anglia Travel Expert*. Under that it said *Ask Me Anything*.

"What's the second highest waterfall in South America?" asked Tom, holding out his ticket.

"I beg your pardon?" said the guard.

"What's the second highest waterfall in South America?" repeated Tom, eyes wide with fake innocence.

"Arguably the Gocta Cataracts in Peru at seven hundred and seventy one metres," she replied. "But it's disputed. Would you like me to go into more detail, sir?"

"Er, no," stammered Tom, going red.

"Fine," said the guard. She glanced under the table. Dave growled. "Keep that dog off the seat, please, and enjoy your journey."

As the guard moved along the carriage, Richard brushed imaginary crumbs from his skinny jeans and gave Tom a sideways glare. "That was embarrassing," he observed. He looked at Orla. "Right, what does this top-secret letter say?"

"Uncle Valentine says if we miss the 18.50 Coasthopper bus from King's Lynn we'll have to sleep in the cemetery," said Orla. "And we're to let ourselves into the house because he'll be out on the mussel shoals until moonrise.

The generator is in the rope-house ... blah-blah ... over the bridge ... blah ... turn key ... waffle ... green button ... et cetera ... understood."

"You what?" Richard snatched the letter from Orla's hand and scanned it with a rapidly deepening frown. "What are mussel shoals?"

"Places where mussels live," said Orla.

Richard looked at Tom. "He's a nutter," he said.

Tom nodded. He agreed completely.

After she'd chosen a holiday with Uncle Valentine – whom she'd last seen when she was six – Orla had spent a fortnight studying maps of the territory. Sicow's Creek stood alone in a vast tract of salt marsh with the North Sea on one side and woodland on the other. But there were clues in the surrounding place names that made her uneasy. Too many saints' names. Too many ancient monuments and sacred spaces.

Orla sighed, her breath fogging the window. Up until last summer she'd been fearless, or so she thought: happy to throw herself into any situation just to see what happened. She had always been curious, impatient and easily bored. Orla believed that life was a pretty amazing story and was scared only by the thought of not being part of it.

Last August, though, her tendency to blunder in without a plan had very nearly doomed the entire family. The discovery of an amazing treasure in a Cornish wood had led her into a dark world of witchcraft and mortal danger, and pretty much the only reason she'd survived was curled up at her feet, his nose carefully tucked into his bum.

Orla reached beneath the table to stroke Dave's head. He sighed, and she smiled, dragging herself back to a world where Richard and Tom were happily reminding each other of incidents that proved Uncle Valentine's eccentricity. Or Great-Uncle Valentine, technically speaking, since he was Dad's dad's brother.

Tom grinned. "Remember the story about when his trousers caught fire?"

"Or when the wheel came off the sidecar he built and he crashed his motorbike into that lady's greenhouse?"

Tom giggled. "Didn't he build a submarine once?"

Richard nodded. "The one that went down but couldn't come up? The coastguard helicopter rescued him. It was on the news."

"See?" said Orla, grabbing the letter back from her older brother. "It's got to be more exciting than watching TV at Gran's house."

"One request, though," said Richard. He checked over his shoulder to make sure no one was listening. "That stick of yours gives me the creeps, so can we make a deal?"

"It's called a gwelen, and I only brought it in case of an emergency. But yes, I'm listening."

"No witchy stuff, please. Let's just have a normal holiday."

"Total deal." Orla nodded. She wanted nothing more.

Under the table, Dave uncurled and stretched. It was impossible to get any sleep with all the giggling and prodding, and as head of household security and close protection specialist, he needed to see where he was going. He jumped up on the seat, then onto the table to admire the view, wiping dog snot all over the window.

"Dave," they all hissed.

Orla laid down her coat to protect the seat and dragged him down to sit beside her. "You're getting heavy, dog," she muttered.

"He's out of shape," said Tom. "Too many pies."

"Too much screen time," added Richard.

Dave felt himself getting hot under the collar. People always spoke about him as though he wasn't there. But it was true: he had indeed spent much of the past few months lying on the sofa with Orla watching telly. He liked nature programmes, fly-on-the-wall documentaries about policemen and old Road Runner cartoons.

"He deserves to take it easy," said Richard. "He's, like, fifty-six in human terms."

"Fifty-six?" cried Orla. She covered Dave's ears. "Don't listen to them, dog. You're more like thirty-six."

"That's still old," said Tom.

They had to run to catch the 18.50 bus from King's Lynn, and the rain started falling as they rode east along the coast road. By the time they reached Taylan Mill – the nearest stop to Sicow's Creek – they were the only passengers left on the bus.

Orla was first off. The rain had passed and as she stood in the lane, she was hit by a gust of excitement at being somewhere new and unexplored. It was a familiar feeling: a tingling that started in her toes and crept up her spine to the nape of her neck. This, thought Orla, had to be the reason why explorers could never settle down. But there was something else, lurking at the back of her mind, like unfinished homework. A sense that her arrival had somehow been noticed. She tried her best to shake it off. Paranoia wasn't a good look.

"Middle of flipping nowhere," sighed Richard, gazing up at the orange and purple sky. "Exactly as expected." He frowned at the bright white light to the west. "Is that a stadium out there in the swamp?"

"Why can't we have holidays like normal people?" muttered Tom.

Dave held his nose high, sniffing the air for clues. There was no shortage of intriguing smells. Salt, deer, fox, pheasant, rabbit, stagnant water, something dead – badger, probably – rotting fish, weird poo, diesel and a faint smell of burning. He sneezed and shook his head, tugging on the lead.

"We're going to die of boredom," moaned Tom.

"You said that about Cornwall," pointed out Orla, "and you soon changed your mind."

Tom shuddered. "We agreed never to talk of Cornwall," he said solemnly.

Richard was holding his phone above his head in the strange way people do when they think an extra few inches will make a difference to reception. "There's one bar and it's not 4G," he said at last. "Which way?"

Orla pointed with her stick. "Down this track and across the salt marsh. It's only a mile."

Richard looked sadly at his wheelie case. Four hours ago, at King's Cross Station, it had been shiny and new. Now it was scuffed and dirty, and in a few minutes, he was going to have to drag it across a marsh. From somewhere in the gathering dusk a tawny owl screeched. Possibly with laughter.

"I'm going to hate it here," he muttered.

Orla was sure that the last time she had seen Uncle Valentine he was living in a normal house, in a village. Now, though, the only buildings visible were four crooked-looking shacks of flint and weatherboard, raised on stilts and silhouetted against the embers of the sun.

15

Uncle Valentine's letter said he had placed oyster shells to mark the path across the marsh. When she'd read it, Orla had wondered how on earth she was going to spot a seashell in the mud, but there they were: small piles that glowed like cats' eyes in the twilight. Dave was in front, using his lead to pull Orla in the right direction. Somewhere to their right, there was the distant sound of waves crashing on an unseen shore. To their left, the easily amused owl; and, every now and then, the indignant quacks of roosting ducks rudely awakened by their footsteps. Ahead, in the distance, that stadium blaze of searing white light that Orla thought was entirely inappropriate for such a deliciously desolate spot.

"Maybe it's a high-security prison," muttered Richard, snatching at his case. There was a nasty cracking sound as the handle broke, then a soft squelch and a cry of shocked indignation.

Orla sighed. Her brother's bag lay on its back in a pool of mud, like a happy piglet.

"Seriously?" wailed Richard, as though questioning a cruel god. The bag made a sucking noise as he dragged it from the mud and the three plodded on silently, like exhausted fugitives. At last they were there. Almost.

"Is one of those Uncle Valentine's actual house?" gasped Tom as it became clear that the dilapidated cabins they'd seen on the horizon were to be their home for the week. "I thought they were ruins."

"Must be," said Orla. "Uncle Valentine said we had to turn the generator on to get power. It's in that shed over the bridge."

"Off you go, then," said Richard. "We'll wait here."

Orla bent to release Dave's lead, allowing him to carry out his risk assessment. He tiptoed across the bridge, his nose swinging left and right. When he stopped, Orla followed, over the ditch and up three steep steps to pull open the door. The generator, with its key and its big green button, was exactly where Uncle Valentine had said it would be. She turned the key to 1, pushed the button and watched lights flicker on in the house. It was such a thrill to be here, with days and days of exploration ahead, that she felt a rush of relief. Worrying was pointless.

Like the generator shed, the house itself stood above the ground on thick trunks of bog oak. Richard was first to mount the steps up to the green door.

"This is an exceptionally cool house," said Orla, peering into the gloom beneath.

"We should knock," advised Richard.

"Orla said he was out," replied Tom.

"I know," said Richard. "But you don't just go breaking in— Oh. Apparently you do."

Orla had barged past him, entering a kitchen with a low ceiling and a wooden floor. In the middle of the huge table, next to a bottle of rum, was a cardboard box with the word WELCOME written in big black letters.

"Crisps," announced Tom, peering inside the box as Orla locked the door. "And choccy and Dairylea triangles and Fanta and something in a brown bag ... oh. Apples." He pushed the bag to one side. "Biscuits. Monster Munch. Strawberry milk..."

"Anything for Dave?" asked Orla. She looked around. "Where is he?"

"He went upstairs to check for hostiles," said Richard. He had mud in his hair and salt stains on his suede shoes, but no one thought it was a good idea to tell him. He popped a can of Fanta and took a long swig.

"Nice clock," he belched, running his fingers over a timepiece the size of a breeze block perched precariously on top of a narrow mahogany display case. It was just past 9.35 p.m., and outside night had fallen. "Looks like jade. Must be worth a packet." He reached out to touch the clock then jumped backwards as the display case went into an alarming wobble.

"Careful," warned Orla. "It's too early to be smashing up the place."

She leaned her stick against the wall and grabbed an

apple. It was soft and wrinkly, and smelled of wet grass. She rubbed it on her T-shirt, took a bite and pulled the Manila envelope from her pocket.

"Our rooms are named after birds," she said. "Tom's in Coot; I'm in Nightjar; Richard, you're in Greylag."

"Best get the disappointment out of the way, then," sighed Richard. He headed for the stairs, followed by Tom. Orla unpacked Dave's rations from her backpack – a value pack of Kitekat Fish Megamix in jelly – then followed.

Dave was already in Nightjar, sniffing along the skirting boards as though he smelled a rat, his claws clicking on the floorboards. Orla dropped her backpack on the pink bedspread. A pile of books stood on the bedside table, topped by *The Sunshine Story Book for Girls*. The cover showed a rosy-cheeked girl with a flower in her hair hugging a soppy-looking Labrador. Orla raised an eyebrow. She switched off the light so she could see the night sky, but if there were any stars, they were too weak to punch through the white glare in the west.

"Horrible light pollution," she muttered to Dave. "Think of all the energy they're wasting."

She reached into her backpack and pulled out a rag doll. It was no ordinary rag doll. This was Malasana, a crazy-haired gypsy in a torn dress. She came from Madrid, had magical powers and had once worked with Dave to save

19

Orla's life. You didn't leave a doll like that at home when you went travelling.

Orla looked first at Malasana, then at Dave. "Feels pretty safe here," she whispered. "But you never know."

She dug into her backpack again and pulled out a tattered red notebook held together with sticky tape. Its front cover was adorned with a childish yet intricate pentagram, a five-pointed star, and surrounded by curious symbols drawn in silver Sharpie. A book of handwritten spells, collected and carefully recorded by a Cornish peller – or witch – called Miss Teague and given to Orla as a gift of protection. Better to have it and not need it than need it and not have it, Orla always thought.

She removed her spare clothes, her wash kit and a velvet bag containing a dried toad, a snakeskin her dad had sent from Africa, the bleached skull of a hare and a crow's feather. These things were among the essentials if you suddenly needed to perform a conjuring or prepare a blasting so, like the spell book, she'd brought them just in case. They couldn't be left lying around, though, so she hid them in the back of the bedside drawer, then slid her gwelen under the bed.

A gwelen was a heavy staff of sacred wood – blackthorn in Orla's case, but ash, beech or willow worked well too – that acted like a kind of vacuum cleaner, sucking up and storing the powerful earth energy that witches call sprowl, as essential to their craft as oxygen is to life. But Orla doubted she'd need it here. Sprowl didn't like the sea. Nor did proper witches. All of which was pretty comforting.

She checked the window again. The bright white light in the west reflected in the pools and along the creeks across the marsh and she felt a rush of sympathy for all the birds trying to roost out there. It must be like trying to get to sleep with the bedroom light still on, she thought.

"C'mon, dog," she said, taking a deep breath. "Let's check on the others."

She put her head around Coot's door. Tom was stretched out on the bed, gazing in awe at a ledge that ran along the wall just below the ceiling.

"There's a railway," he cried. "Look – it goes all around the room and through a tunnel."

Orla glanced up. Mountains were painted on the doors of a huge wooden wardrobe and the railway passed through a painted arch to run through the wardrobe. It emerged from the other side, passed through a miniature forest and disappeared between the half-timbered houses of what looked like a German village.

"Awesome," marvelled Orla. "But where's the train?"

Tom lifted up a shoebox with the words *Fix me* on the side. "In here. Must be broken."

In Greylag Richard was sitting miserably on his bed.

"My shoes are ruined," he moaned. "Salt ruins suede. And this mattress is too hard." He thumped the bed to prove his point.

Orla ignored him and studied the room. There was a box of assorted electronic components on the bare wood floor and a big black screen. "What happened to the TV?"

Richard gave her a sad look and held up a yellow Post-it note. It said *Fix me*.

"Might be a bit beyond your skill set," Orla said with a grin. "Maybe help Tom mend his toy train first."

"You're funny. What did you get?"

She frowned. "An inappropriate book."

There was a gruff shout from downstairs. "You lot up there?"

"Uncle Valentine!" cried Orla. She dashed for the stairs, almost tripping as Dave raced past her, barking like a maniac. Orla sped after him, desperate not to let the holiday start with one of Dave's friendly fire incidents.

She needn't have worried. An enormous man with a red face and a wild beard, dressed like he'd chosen his outfit from a bin at the back of a charity shop, was lying on his back on the kitchen floor, his eyes wide open and staring unblinking at the ceiling. His reaction had confused Dave, who knew that dead bodies should always be considered booby-trapped until proven otherwise. He sniffed the corpse suspiciously.

"Works with bears and Jack Russells," said the corpse as Dave leapt backwards.

Orla smiled. "Hello, Uncle Valentine."

The corpse sat up, eyes still wide and mouth now open. "Orla Perry?"

She nodded. "Pleased to meet you."

"*The* Orla Perry?"

"The very same."

"Can't be," said the corpse. "First off, my great-niece Orla Perry is about this high…" He held his hand at the height of a six-year-old. "And secondly, she had hair as red as mine right down her back." He squinted at Orla. "You're too tall, and your hair's shorter."

"Hello, Uncle Valentine," said Tom, pushing past Orla.

"Yes, hi," added Richard warily from behind his sister.

The huge man studied their faces, then shook his head. "You're all impostors, but I can't throw you out on a night like this." He pulled himself to his feet, stooping as though accustomed to colliding with the ceiling.

"Who's that?" he asked, pointing at Dave.

"Dave T. Dog," said Orla.

Uncle Valentine bent and gave the Jack Russell an affectionate pat that was so hard it made Dave's eyes water.

"What's the T stand for?" asked Uncle Valentine.

"THE," they yelled in unison.

"Very funny." Uncle Valentine nodded, then clapped his hands. "Now, pay attention because I'm only going to tell you this once." He began to rotate, pointing with both fingers like a gun turret. "Kitchen – keep clean and tidy at all times. Knives in drawers, plates in cupboards. Fireplace – kindling in the basket, matches on the mantelpiece, logs outside. The TV was there but it won't work until Richard fixes it, and over there's my Afghan rug: it's very valuable, so don't drop jam on it. Past the stairs is the front room. I only use it when the vicar comes visiting."

"How often is that?" asked Orla.

"Never," replied Uncle Valentine. "But you need to be prepared." He pointed at a large globe on a gleaming brass stand. "That's my second most treasured possession, so treat it with care. The dots on it are the places I've been. And that..." He pointed at the wobbly clock. "That is my number one most treasured possession. It's made of jade from China and used to belong to an emperor, so best not to touch. You'll note that it's balanced on an alarmingly precarious surface."

"Why don't you move it somewhere safer?" asked Tom.

Uncle Valentine rubbed his beard. "Because if I put it anywhere else it stops working, and I need it to work because it's a lifesaver."

"A lifesaver?" asked Richard. "Because it tells the time?"

"Not exactly," said Uncle Valentine. He held a finger in the air. All was silent but for the ticking of the emperor's clock. Then, at 10 p.m. on the dot, it emitted a weedy tinkle. Uncle Valentine laughed with glee. "Every time I hear that chime, I can pour myself a tot of rum. That's why it's a lifesaver."

He grabbed the bottle from the kitchen table, pulled the cork out with his teeth, poured a shot and swallowed it in one gulp.

"Ah!" He smiled, wiping his mouth with the back of his hand. "Now, where was I? Oh, yes – the outbuildings. There's the rope-house just over the footbridge, with the generator, rescue gear and fuel."

"Rescue gear?" asked Tom.

"Throwing lines, torches, life jackets, that sort of thing," explained Uncle Valentine. "They're treacherous waters out there, and when you live this close to them you need to be prepared."

He rubbed his beard. "Now then, the big building after that with the ramp is the workshop. Lots of power tools and sharp things in there, so be careful. The far one is the smokehouse. Stay well out of there. Oh, and you'll probably want the code for the high-speed fibre-optic Internet."

Richard turned his eyes to heaven and let out silent thanks. Tom just breathed, "Yes, please."

25

"Thought you would." Uncle Valentine nodded. "But there isn't one."

"No code?" asked Richard, already swiping his phone.

"No Internet." Uncle Valentine grinned. "You'll live."

He went to the back door, then turned. "Who wants fish and chips?" he asked.

"Yay!" they cried, but their joy was cut short as Uncle Valentine returned to drop four very fresh, very shiny and very raw haddock and a dozen uncooked potatoes on the table.

"Better get peeling, boys," he said. "Orla can make the batter while I heat the oil."

"Why does Orla get to make the batter?" asked Tom.

Uncle Valentine smiled. "Because she's the lady of the house."

First the soppy books for girls. Now the cooking. "Actually, I'm rubbish at cooking," sniffed Orla. "Richard is the master chef. I'll do the peeling."

Uncle Valentine raised an eyebrow. "Fair enough," he said. He turned to Tom. "How's your sister ever going to find a husband if she can't cook?"

There was a spluttering, slightly squeaky sound from beside the cooker. It was Richard bursting into a fit of giggles.

*   *   *

Exactly ninety minutes later Richard put down his knife and fork, sat back in his chair and rubbed his belly. "That, without doubt, was the best fish and chips I've ever had."

"Or ever will have," agreed Tom, collecting the plates.

"I'm stuffed," said Orla.

"So's your hound," said Uncle Valentine, nodding towards a very fat, very happy Jack Russell. "We'll have to run that flab off him this week."

Dave's contentment evaporated in a long sigh.

Uncle Valentine opened a drawer in the kitchen table and pulled out a rolled-up document. "This here's the Admiralty chart for this part of the coast," he said. He unrolled it, weighing down the corners with salt, pepper, ketchup and vinegar. "Gather round while I show you the lie of the land. This here's Sicow's Creek. All around us, tidal salt marsh. Beyond this line of dunes to the north is Stubborn Sands; and over here to the east, the valley of the Swallow River. She's the most beautiful chalk stream in the county and tidal for the last mile and a half. There's good fishing at her mouth but you can't follow her upstream any more and you mustn't be out after dark. You need to be indoors, with the lights on. Got it?"

"Why?" asked Orla. She was genuinely curious.

Uncle Valentine looked at her, then at the boys, as though trying to decide how much to tell them.

"The dyke paths are slippery," he said at last. "And the creeks are deep. People disappear on the marsh all the time. Bodies are sometimes found, but mostly the sea keeps them."

The clock ticked. The wind rattled the windows. Dave ate a dead fly. Eventually Richard broke the silence.

"You're joking, right?"

Uncle Valentine shook his head. "No, I'm not. And there's another thing. You might hear the Drowning Bell. Ding … ding … ding it goes, from a submerged church far out at sea. If you hear it, someone you love is drowning. So don't be out in the dark, stay out of the water and you'll be safe. Daylight is a different matter." He placed an oil-stained finger on the map, tracking the Swallow River upstream to a perfect circle of woodland. "Except here. This is Anna's Wood, and it's out of bounds." He gave them a stern look. "I mean put-you-on-the-next-bus-home out of bounds."

"Fine," said Orla, unconvincingly. "What are all those lights to the west?"

Uncle Valentine's face darkened. "The Devil's work is what. It's the GasFrac compound where they keep their infernal machines." He jabbed his stubby, oily finger violently at the map. "All this – the marsh, the dunes, the beach, the workshop here at Sicow's Creek – is your

28

playground during the day, but Anna's Wood, the GasFrac compound and the smokehouse are off limits. Get it?"

The gang nodded solemnly.

Orla planned to go to Anna's Wood as soon as possible.

"What's GasFrac?" asked Tom.

"They're a drilling company," explained Richard. "They pump chemicals and water into the bedrock to release natural gas. It's all quite controversial."

As the emperor's clock chimed midnight, Uncle Valentine poured two inches of rum into a glass and took a long, angry swig. "Controversial?" he spluttered. "It's criminal. They've discovered shale gas in the rocks under Anna's Wood and by nefarious means they've got permission from everyone who matters to drill a well and pump the stuff out." He took another swig of rum, his hand shaking with anger. "Three thousand years that wood's been there. Ancient Britons, Iceni, Romans, Saxons and Vikings have all worshipped nature there, and yet for the sake of gas that'll be burned away in a year, the wood has to go."

"What do you mean *go*?" asked Richard.

"I mean go as in chainsawed, bulldozed, ploughed up and concreted over," muttered Uncle Valentine. "Those devils move in a week Monday." He slammed down his glass. "But it's not your business. Now get to bed. It's gone midnight."

"Sweet dreams, everyone," said Richard, and Uncle Valentine gave a hollow laugh.

"All we dream of around here is a shopping centre and a country park," he said.

CHAPTER 2

At 5.15 a.m. the entire salt marsh woke up, with ducks, geese, waders, warblers and divers ruffling their feathers and yelling at the sun to hurry up and rise. Orla opened her eyes, touched the silver star she wore around her neck for luck, then dashed to the window. The eastern horizon was a streak of pink, the west a wall of white light against the fleeing night.

Dave stood up, yawned and began his morning yoga routine: downward dog, cat-cow, baby cobra.

"Dawn patrol, dog," whispered Orla.

She snapped Dave into his black tactical harness, then dressed herself in shorts, a green jumper and socks that almost matched. She grabbed her gwelen from under the bed, and paused. It was force of habit, but she didn't need it because this morning she was just going for a walk like a normal person. Not collecting sprowl like a witch. After all, she'd made a deal with Richard. She shoved the gwelen back under the bed, then pulled it out again. Dave yawned.

On second thoughts, what harm was there in taking it along?

Orla and Dave tiptoed downstairs and into the kitchen. Uncle Valentine was asleep in a chair beside the cold fireplace, his mouth wide open and an empty bottle of rum beside him. Orla turned to Dave, put a finger to her lips and crept towards the back door.

"Going somewhere, girl?" asked Uncle Valentine, his eyes still closed.

"Taking Dave for his early morning walk," she whispered.

Opening his eyes, Uncle Valentine glanced at the emperor's clock and raised an eyebrow.

"Early riser, aren't you?"

Orla nodded. "Best part of the day."

"True," he agreed. "Did you see the books I left out for you? Lots of activities for girls in them."

"Not for this girl," she muttered.

"Please yourself. Where you headed?"

"Just exploring."

"On your own?" Uncle Valentine's eyes widened. He looked worried. Presumably he'd thought that Orla would be happy to spend the day embroidering a cushion cover.

"I'm not on my own, Uncle Valentine," said Orla sweetly. "I've got my dog to protect me." She bent down to give Dave a hug like that girl on the cover of *The Sunshine Story Book for Girls*. Dave growled. Then farted.

Orla picked up the binoculars from the windowsill. "Can I borrow these?"

"What for?"

"Birdwatching?"

Uncle Valentine nodded. "Don't lose them," he said. "What's that pole you've got there?"

Orla smiled innocently. "A walking stick."

"Is it indeed?" muttered Uncle Valentine. He didn't sound convinced. "You stay out of that wood."

Dave took off like a bullet, sniffing, weeing and rolling his way across the marsh. Orla followed, grinning so hard that her face hurt. She loved the feeling of being the first person to see the day, especially somewhere new. The air smelled of salt, mud and sea lavender and the musty dampness of the low grey mist that was draped over the creeks. She paused on the footbridge and gazed across the marsh, past the rotting timbers of a mud-stranded fishing boat to the dunes and the salt haze beyond. Dave had yet another wee, then trotted ahead to roll in goose poo. It made sense, he reasoned, to blend in with the surroundings.

Together they wandered along the path they'd followed last night, eventually reaching the coast road. Dave was cautiously optimistic about this new area of operations. As close protection specialist and head of household security to the Perry family, his life involved long periods of risk assessment and tactical planning punctuated with brief moments of extreme anxiety – especially when he was with the girl. But here felt, well, good. He looked up at Orla, wagging his tail.

"What?"

Dave sneezed, then barked.

"I get it," she cried, bending down to pat him, spotting the goose poo and changing her mind. "You're happy to be on holiday too, right?"

Dave shook himself, the tremor starting at his whiskers and travelling to the tip of his tail and back. He was never on holiday.

To the left the road dipped, descending to a stone bridge that lay in a pool of mist dusted pink by the sun. Dave jumped onto the parapet and stared down through the swirl to where the water ran beneath. Orla joined him.

"That's the Swallow River," she said. "The most beautiful chalk stream in the county." She lifted her head, her gaze following the misty valley south to a distant copse on what looked like a miniature hill. "And that must be Anna's Wood." She glanced back towards Sicow's Creek, then at Dave. "Are you thinking what I'm thinking?"

There was a path alongside the river but it was blocked by an orange plastic barrier. *Path closed*, announced one sign. *No right of way*, said another. *No trespassing*, warned a third, while a fourth stated: *CCTV in operation*.

None of the above deterred Orla in the slightest as she slipped past the barrier and headed upstream along the overgrown path. Dave pushed past her to take point, tunnelling through the undergrowth and hopping over fallen branches.

Ahead, Anna's Wood appeared as a dark green dome in a shallow valley of pale green barley fields: a tiny hillock that looked as though it had grown up in the wrong place.

Suddenly Dave stopped, one paw held high and his tail rigid. Orla crouched down.

"What is it?" she whispered.

Dave was staring at a silver birch on the opposite bank, and it took Orla a few seconds to see the blinking red light of the CCTV camera.

"Don't worry," she murmured. "Who's going to be watching a camera pointed at an empty field at six o'clock in the morning?"

Dave strongly disagreed with Orla's risk assessment and veered into the field, staying low in the barley. Orla followed, enjoying the adventure.

Their infiltration ended where a ten-foot chain-link

security fence with barbed wire along the top encircled the wood. Yellow signs were attached at twenty-five-yard intervals, the smiley green GasFrac logo at odds with the message:

**PRIVATE PROPERTY. NO TRESPASSING.
THIS AREA IS PATROLLED. CCTV IN OPERATION.
DO NOT ENTER. WE WILL PROSECUTE.**

Like a prisoner, Orla peered through the wire at the mysterious Anna's Wood. It was somehow magical in an inexplicable way: a bump in the earth of soaring beeches and spreading oaks bisected by the babbling Swallow River. A geological conjuring trick made even stranger, thought Orla, because the river had cut its way through the hill rather than simply flowing around. And the birdsong – the glorious finale to the dawn chorus – seemed more anxious than joyful, as though the birds feared the sun might never rise again. She gripped her gwelen, glad now that she'd brought it along.

Something flickered, and then it was gone, like a blank frame in a filmstrip. It wasn't in Anna's Wood and it wasn't in her head. It was somewhere in between. And there it was again – gone in a flash and leaving her off balance. Orla looked at Dave. He hadn't seen it, but then he wouldn't. He was a dog. Mostly.

"This wood needs exploring," she whispered, "but there's no way in."

Dave yawned. There was always a way in. Slinking through the long grass at the woodland edge, he followed the fence back to the river, staying low until he was sure there were no more cameras. The fence ended at the water's edge, then continued on the far bank. In between, three lengths of barbed wire had been stretched across the river. All they had to do was step into the river and wade – or swim, in Dave's case – under the spikes.

Once inside the fence and under the woodland canopy, Orla felt as though she were standing in a cathedral. The trees soared like columns, the leaves scattered the sunlight like stained glass and in place of the choir, the alarm calls of blackbirds, thrushes, blackcaps and robins echoed like the prayers of the desperate.

Hands on hips, Orla stood on the riverbank, looking around for clues like an explorer in an unmapped jungle. Upstream, a kingfisher flashed like a blue bullet while overhead a flock of magpies chattered like machine guns. The wildlife was skittish. Nervous. Fearful, even.

Dave trotted to an oak tree and tried to leap onto a lower branch. It took him three attempts but he finally made it and perched there, looking exceedingly pleased with himself.

Orla shook her head. "I wish you'd stop that," she sighed. "Dogs aren't supposed to climb trees. What if someone saw?"

Her portly Jack Russell wouldn't be quite so smug if he knew he'd gained his feline superpowers from the magic cat medicine she'd used to bring him back to life in Cornwall, she thought. She shuddered at the memory.

Dave wasn't listening. He was staring into the leaves, trying to locate the source of an urgent fluttering that sounded like two pigeons fighting.

Orla spun in a circle, taking everything in.

"Can you feel it?" she murmured.

It was a daft question because there was nothing to feel. Just an absence. She stabbed the tip of her gwelen into the carpet of leaves, waiting to feel the pulse-like throb and gentle heat as sprowl was absorbed, but all she felt was the shiny bark of a dead stick. She looked around, searching for clues. Birds, trees, wild garlic, moss, running water, a drift of bluebells, and all somehow brighter, stronger and more beautiful, as though seen through a filter.

Dave craned his neck. There was a rope running up the tree trunk towards the fluttering. It was taut, as though it was weighted.

"There's no sprowl," whispered Orla. Not even a dribble, and that was odd.

38

Sprowl can't be used up, like coal or gold. It's an infinite resource, generated by the earth's rotation and running in swirling subterranean currents that are known by many different names. The Polynesians call it mana; the Bushmen, n'om. The Chinese, qi; and the ancient Incas knew it as ukhu pacha. But wherever you are, the force is so abundant that, for those with the talent, finding it is easy. It seeps out from cracks in the earth, is sucked up by the roots of trees and bushes – blackthorn, yew and holm oak especially – and is attracted to places where forces collide, such as crossroads and where waters meet. Gathering sprowl to power magic was ninety-eight per cent of a witch's work, but it was like panning for gold: you could spend a lifetime collecting a flake here, a grain there, but you'd never be rich.

This weird wood, thought Orla, gazing at the glassy river and the ancient trees, looked like a likely spot. But there was an echoing emptiness, as though whatever energy had come here had been turned away, the subterranean river somehow dammed. It was deeply disappointing, but since she'd broken a promise to her brothers, it was probably no more than she deserved.

Plus, a dearth of sprowl meant an absence of witches – apart from her – and that was a good thing.

Up in the tree, Dave's ears pricked up. He switched his

gaze to the perimeter fence. A low warning growl came from deep in his belly, his tail pointing straight up and the fur on his neck like a porcupine. Trouble was coming. He couldn't see them yet, but his nose and ears had detected two men and a dog. A German shepherd. Textbook security patrol with radios to call in reinforcements. He threw a look at Orla and leapt from the tree. It was time to go.

"Wait," said Orla. A single black feather had spiralled from the oak to the woodland floor. She picked it up and gazed into the tree and there, in a tiny gap between the leaves, she saw the cage. That fluttering wasn't caused by squabbling pigeons.

"It's a magpie, dog," she gasped. "Can you see? It's caught in a trap."

Dave looked up, catching a glimpse of a steel cage hanging from the rope. A radio crackled – worryingly close by – and he heard an excited yelp as the guard dog picked up the scent trail. Orla was looking for a way to scale the tree, but there was no time.

"Woof," said Dave softly – translation *let's get the heck out of here* – but Orla ignored him. If she could just get onto that first branch the rest would be easy. It was too far to jump but there was another way. Dave had got up there – eventually – by running up the trunk. Maybe she could do the same.

The security detail was a hundred and fifty yards away, studying the tracks Orla had left in the grass when she climbed out of the river. The German shepherd was getting agitated.

"Ace has smelled something, Trev," grunted one of the guards, who looked as though he'd been thrown out of jail for being too mean.

The other guard followed the dog's gaze, to where Orla was backing up for her run. He looked even tougher. "There's someone there!" he growled, unsnapping the lead. "Get them, Ace."

As Orla sprinted at the tree, the guard dog accelerated like a guided missile, reaching one side of the trunk as Orla's left foot hit the other. Dave looked up at Orla, then at the German shepherd, and decided that in a situation like this there was only one thing he could do. He yelped like a frightened puppy and ran away as fast as his short legs could carry him. As Orla pushed herself upwards, Ace ran below, his head down like a hunting wolf. Grabbing at branches, Orla hauled herself into the tree and looked down to see the shaved heads of the security men following their dog.

"That was close," she muttered, clambering towards the cage. It was a simple affair with a trapdoor that was tripped when the prey went for the bait – a dead rabbit in this case. As Orla came near, the black and white bird stopped struggling and gazed at her with glittering eyes, hopping backwards and forward on a single foot.

"What happened to your foot, little magpie?" asked Orla. She shook her head. "Never mind – you can tell me later. First I need to get you out of here."

Hooking her feet around the branch to keep herself steady, she reached in with both hands, grabbed the bird and gently pulled her from the cage. She felt tiny in her hands, her magpie heart beating so fast Orla was scared she might die of fright. She raised the bird and looked her in the eye.

"I'm not going to hurt you," she whispered, relaxing her grip. "See? You're free."

The magpie opened her wings, leapt forward and stabbed Orla's cheek with her sharp beak.

"You call that gratitude?" yelped Orla as the bird flashed into the wood.

Dave was exhausted. His tongue hanging out like a rasher of bacon, he lay on his side in the long grass at the edge of the barley field, panting like a freight train. He'd only got away because the guards had called off the chase. It was a good thing the German shepherd was so disciplined, because Dave really didn't want to speculate what would have happened in paw-to-paw combat between thirty-five kilos of fighting fit German shepherd and nine – OK, ten – kilos of tired old Jack Russell.

He sniffed the air and cautiously, painfully, got to his paws. Orla was walking along the field edge, one hand on her left cheek and the other dragging her gwelen.

She smiled, bending down to pat him. Blood dripped onto the grass. "Nice work, dog. Diversionary action to draw the enemy force away from the focus of operations. Beautifully executed."

Dave put his front paws gently on her arm and stretched up to lick her cheek. He wasn't just a tactical genius. He was a trained medic too.

CHAPTER 3

"Orla got attacked by a magpie," crowed Tom as the kids sat down for lunch – fish paste sandwiches and tea – with Uncle Valentine. He'd spent the morning teaching the boys how to service an outboard motor.

"She only had one foot," said Orla after she'd explained herself.

Uncle Valentine nodded. "Sounds about right. Captains are always getting themselves into tricky situations. She probably lost the foot in a witching trap." He poured water from the kettle into a bowl then opened a cupboard and lifted out a biscuit tin marked with a red cross.

"A what trap?" asked Orla, suddenly wary.

"A witching trap," repeated Uncle Valentine. He opened the tin. It smelled of disinfectant. "You take the hair from a horse's tail and make it into a snare that you tie into a tree. When a bird steps in, the noose pulls tight and traps it."

"Why's it called a witching trap?" asked Tom, as Richard threw Orla a look that said *please, no; not again.*

"Because witches use them, I suppose," said Uncle Valentine, tearing a wad of cotton wool. "They use bits and pieces of birds and reptiles and hares and stuff in their workings, I've heard."

"Was the cage a witching trap?" asked Orla.

"That would have been a Larsen trap. Horrible thing. But used by pest controllers and gamekeepers. Not witches."

Uncle Valentine peered at Orla's wound, half humming, half singing in a low, melodious voice.

> "'The magpie is the murder bird,
> Her soul impelled to kill.
> She brings you luck when from the right
> But from left bodes ill...'"

"What's that?" asked Richard.

"It's a folk song," muttered Uncle Valentine, rinsing the swab in yet more disinfectant.

"Why did you call the bird a captain?" asked Tom.

Their uncle looked thoughtful. "I don't rightly know," he admitted. "But whenever you see one on your left side, you have to salute and say 'Morning, Captain' or 'Afternoon, Captain', depending on the time of day."

He put a hand on Orla's head to steady it and continued singing as he cleaned the cut.

"'Chatterpie at your window,
Longtail at your door,
To give her gift
A little kiss
And show what fate's in store.'"

He sat back. "There'll be a scar, but you'll live." He went to the kitchen sink to wash his hands. "Some say a magpie's kiss gives us a vision of the future," he said, wiping his hands on the seat of his trousers. "Others that it gives a glimpse of your death." He took his seat at the table and reached for the teapot. "To be honest, they're ultimately the same thing."

"Lovely," said Orla. "Can't wait."

And she didn't have to.

Orla was dreaming that she was in a creaky second-hand bookshop, searching tall and crooked shelves while dust specks danced in shafts of moonlight. She was looking for a special map but was interrupted when a magpie fluttered in, landed on her shoulder, dug in the talons of her single foot and screeched "Attatatat!"

Orla raised her hand in a reluctant salute. "Good evening, Captain."

The magpie cackled and flew off, and Orla had no choice but to follow. She walked out of the bookshop and into a moonlit marsh where neither ducks roosted nor owls hunted, letting the magpie lead her over a wide road and into a glaring and painful world of electricity and iron. The wildflowers and watercress had been strangled by hogweed, and where the sparkling river once flowed now lay a series of thick metal pipes, enclosed behind a high fence and lit with floodlights. Yellow signs, like the ones she and Dave had ignored yesterday, were attached to the chain links. Beneath the friendly green logo of the GasFrac corporation, they warned trespassers of prosecution and danger to life. A gate swung open and Orla walked through, noticing as she did so that her feet were bare. She was sure she'd been wearing shoes in the bookshop. And where was Dave?

As she followed a road so new it smelled of tar and so black it seemed to absorb the starlight, she searched in vain for Anna's Wood. Where the Swallow River had flowed through that strange low hill now lay terraces of gleaming concrete lit with yellow gas flares. Panic rising in her chest, she ran across the hard ground to a stone wall, four yards high and festooned with GasFrac ads.

Believe in the Power of Dreams, said one. *Energy doesn't have to cost the earth*, said another. But as Orla came closer, the logos changed from green to red, the words dissolved and in the silver moonlight the truth emerged. *Sucking the soul from the planet*, boasted one. *Everyone has their price*, proclaimed another. *Generating the power for profit*, said a third.

Chattering angrily, the magpie fluttered along the wall and perched above another sign. Orla found it was getting hard to breathe, and harder to walk. The air smelled as though the bedrock were on fire and her legs felt as if she were knee-deep in clay. She pushed on. This last sign was blinking on and off like broken neon, but the message was just legible.

IT'S NOT ABOUT THE GAS, FOLKS!

Orla turned to walk away. She was trespassing on somebody else's problem.

"Sorry, magpie," she whispered. "I saved you once but I can't do it again."

The magpie's chatter sounded like a sorrowful laugh as she swooped past Orla to land further along the wall. Another bird joined her, then five more, then twenty, then fifty. There were blue-eyed jackdaws, dopey wood pigeons and nervous blackbirds. They darted out of the darkness to line up like spectators to disaster, the wind from their wings scattering the leaves as they wheeled this way and that in search of a perch. A barn owl landed on a concrete post and a mob of long-tailed tits lined up along a sign saying *Keep Clear*.

Woodpeckers, thrushes, bullfinches with their pink breasts, a pair of red kites, a stonechat and a buzzard flew in – and as each touched down it began to sing, loudly, urgently, as though pleading with Orla to do something she couldn't understand. And there was another sound: like the gasp of an approaching jet. The birds shuffled to face it, their eyes closed and their heads bowed. The sound intensified from a whine to a teeth-shattering scream as ten thousand points of light streaked through the darkness, ripping through their feathers like shrapnel.

Orla awoke as though she'd rolled onto a live wire, sitting bolt upright and breathing hard. The dream was fizzling and fading like a burned-out firework, so she fumbled for the switch on her bedside lamp, grabbed her notebook and wrote down the details:

Concrete

Gas flares

Wall

Chemicals

Birds

Devastation

Death

IT'S NOT ABOUT THE GAS

49

She read the words over and over, then fell back on her pillow and stared at the ceiling. So it wasn't about the gas. She got that. Sort of. But it wasn't about her, either. If she went to war with GasFrac it would be out of choice, not destiny. And it was not a choice she'd be making.

She rolled onto her side, hearing the mattress crackle as though it was filled with straw. The glare of the GasFrac compound lit up the window, so she rolled onto her other side, where the glare from the GasFrac compound lit up the bedroom wall.

Orla growled and sat up. Mala was propped up on the chest of drawers, her shadow thrown in sharp detail across the room. She seemed to be staring.

"Hey," hissed Orla. "It's not my problem."

The tattered Spanish rag doll with the crazy hair said nothing. She just stared. Orla fell back and let out a groan. Then she sat up again.

"Listen to me, Malasana," she said sternly. "There'll be conservationists, anti-fracking protesters, wildlife experts and all sorts of very clever people defending the birds and the animals in that wood. No one gets to chop down ancient woodland in England in the twenty-first century without a very, very good reason, and with all those experts, who needs me to stick my nose in?"

Malasana's silence said it all.

Orla let her head drop onto the scratchy pillow. It was no use. Yes, she could simply draw the curtains against the light but they were too thin to make any difference; and anyway, that would be like letting GasFrac win. She closed her eyes and forced her brain to take her to a happy place, a Christmassy world where tiny flakes of soft white snow were falling from the sky and blanketing the trees. She stuck out her tongue to catch one and her heart sank. They weren't snowflakes. They were feathers.

Those poor birds. What if she was wrong and Mala was right? What if they really did need a kid like Orla to stick her nose in?

She groaned, then sat up again, rubbing her hair distractedly.

"Fine," she muttered at the doll. "You win. Tomorrow I'll go and make sure someone is saving the wood. Then we can get on with our holiday. Now will you let me get some sleep?"

CHAPTER 4

Something was tapping on the bedroom window.

"Oh no," groaned Orla. The bedroom was pink with morning light and the shadows were slipping between the floorboards. She curled into a ball of refusal, throwing the blanket over her head and pulling it tight.

Taptaptaptaptaptaptaptaptaptap...

"Go away," she called. "It's morning."

She peeked out from under the blanket to check that it was the real morning and not a dream one. How could she be sure? Pinching yourself only worked in fairy tales. There was a kid in her class who had a theory that everything was a dream: the entire world, the universe, everyone you knew and everything you ever did, all was conjured by the mind and all there was in the entire continuum of space–time was you...

Taptaptaptaptaptaptaptatatatatatap...

She peeped through a crack in the covers. It was the magpie again, tapping on the glass with something hard and blue. Orla leapt out of bed, no longer caring if this was a dream or reality.

"Good morning, Captain," she muttered. "Now, shoo."

Unfazed, the magpie placed the blue object on the window ledge and swooped away.

"Your way of saying sorry, huh?" Orla called after her. She picked up the gift. It was a tiny stone, the size of her fingernail, quite square and bright blue. She dropped it into a yellow teacup for safekeeping and went down to breakfast, where Uncle Valentine and her brothers appeared to be engrossed in an electronics catalogue.

"Day two and I've already fixed my train," exclaimed Tom. "It was just a loose wire. Now I've got to build the layout."

"Amazing," sighed Orla.

"And we've worked out the problem with the TV," said Richard. "The T-CON board is fried."

"You say that like you actually know what it means," she said, cutting a slice from a warm loaf on the table. "Anyone fancy a bike ride this morning?"

No one replied.

"Gentle spin around the neighbourhood? A little reconnaissance mission?"

Dave began dancing on his hind legs when he heard the word "reconnaissance".

Uncle Valentine was pulling his wellies on. "There's a couple of reasonable ladies' bikes in the workshop," he said.

"I'm not a reasonable lady," muttered Orla, gripping her gwelen tightly and making her exit.

Still chewing her bread, she crossed the footbridge and followed the path past the rope-house to the workshop. Inside, at least nine bikes were heaped against the flint wall, covered in dusty cobwebs. How could a man living alone in the middle of a salt marsh need so many bikes? Orla wondered. One stood out: a black vintage Raleigh with a basket on the front that was perfect for Dave. She dragged it free from the pile and pushed it into the light.

"Let me check those tyres for you," offered Uncle Valentine. He had just hoisted a dripping net of mussels from the water beside the jetty and was shovelling them into a string bag that stood on an old-fashioned scale.

The sun was shining across the marsh and a gentle breeze was rattling the reeds. Dave was lying on the top step, soaking up the sunshine and keeping a close eye on a squad of shifty-looking shoveler ducks who seemed to be planning some mischief.

"I'm fine, thanks," replied Orla. She'd already found a pump and she needed no assistance whatsoever from

Uncle Valentine or anybody else, thank you very much. She leaned the bike against the salt-warped boards of the workshop wall and crouched down to attach the pump.

"There's a compressor in the rope-house," called Uncle Valentine. "It's a lot quicker than a handpump."

"No thanks."

"And you'd better let me adjust the brakes for you," he added. He removed half a scoop of mussels out of the sack, checked the weight, then tied the bag shut with a strip of wire.

"I can do that myself," said Orla through gritted teeth.

"Can you indeed?" Uncle Valentine guffawed.

It took her ten sweaty minutes to inflate the cracked old tyres on the ancient bike, five to find some oil for the rusty chain and three to work out a way to attach her gwelen to the crossbar. The brakes looked fine.

"There's an old biscuit tin full of puncture repair kits on the middle shelf," called Uncle Valentine. "You should take one just in case."

"Tyres seem fine," she replied. "C'mon, dog."

Dave gave the ducks his fiercest stare, stretched, then jumped down the steps and jogged across the bridge to the workshop.

"You're going to ride in the basket," announced Orla, lifting him into the creaking wicker. She swung a leg over the wide leather seat. It was time to make contact with the resistance and find out exactly what GasFrac was up to in Anna's Wood.

The secret to keeping Uncle Valentine's antique bicycle upright was speed. Slowing down to make the right-angled turn where the footpath met the creek, she came dangerously close to toppling into the water. Dave threw her a look of wide-eyed consternation as he scrabbled to stay on board.

"Sorry, dog," said Orla, standing on the pedals to pick up speed. The going got easier when she reached the tarmac road and, after conducting a detailed risk assessment, Dave re-emerged from the depths of the basket.

They rode east along the coast road with the wind on their backs, the smell of blackthorn blossom in their faces and fluffy white clouds scudding overhead. Dave's ears were flapping in the wind and Orla was grinning like a monkey. Her grumpiness had been blown away and she knew exactly why. She'd been scared. There: she'd admitted it. The magpie's kiss had shown her the horror that was coming, and her fear had made it someone else's problem. But now she'd realized that her refusal to stand by and do nothing was stronger than her fear. Maybe she would find good people fighting GasFrac, and maybe she wouldn't, but from now on every bird in Anna's Wood had Orla Perry and Dave T. Dog on their side. And that felt good.

"Look, dog – a windmill," she cried, sweeping the hair from her face.

Taylan Mill rose straight out of the marsh, dazzling white in the morning sunshine, its sails whooshing round like tethered pterodactyls. The bike was going quite fast now, thought Dave. Fast enough for it to hurt if anything went wrong. He dug his claws into the wicker but kept smiling, like a scared kid on a grown-up rollercoaster.

"Don't worry," called Orla. "I'm in perfect control."

They sped down a gentle slope towards a humpback bridge, Orla pedalling as fast as she could so they could climb the other side.

"Do you think we can get air?" she panted.

The bike was heavy – built for comfort rather than acrobatics – but if she pulled the bars at the apex of the bridge she thought she could probably get both wheels off the ground. Dave sank into the basket and put his paws over his eyes as the girl who had been scared to leave the house for the past seven months whooped into the April sky.

She managed a tiny jump on the humpback bridge, but the stunt cost her the speed she needed to coast up the other side. They came to a junction with a signpost. St Stannard was two miles straight on; Haddenham St Taylan was two miles to the right, up and over a long, painful-looking hill. A trio of magpies – three for a girl –

settled on the Haddenham arm, staring at Orla and Dave like gangsters. Dave showed them some teeth. They were utterly unimpressed.

"Which way?" asked Orla.

Dave looked right, up the hill. That would slow her down, and hopefully tire her out. He barked, and Orla nodded, standing up to pedal the heavy bicycle over the hill. Dave glanced back. The magpies weren't following. He looked ahead. It was a very long way to the top. He was just thinking about how it wasn't too bad being a passenger when the bike suddenly stopped.

"Out, dog," panted Orla. "You need the exercise."

Dave glanced at the hill, then at Orla. Seriously? He jumped reluctantly from the basket. It was indeed a very long way to the top.

"Race you," called Orla, pedalling away.

Astonishingly, Dave beat her, arriving at the summit with enough time to get his breath back and regain his dignity before Orla arrived, her cheeks red and chest heaving from the exertion.

"Wow," she gasped, twisting to take in the view. To the south, nestled in a copse, was the village that Orla recognized from the map as Haddenham St Taylan. To the east was a patchwork of fields in browns, greens and mustard yellow; and to the north lay the salt marsh, the sea and the offshore wind farm. North-west, thirty-five miles across the Wash, were the loops of the rollercoaster at Ingoldmells in Lincolnshire, and in the west she could see Sicow's Creek and the beach. Beyond it was the GasFrac compound with the yellow earth movers and bulldozers lined up like the tanks of an invading army. Below lay the Swallow Valley and the strange little hill that was Anna's Wood.

"Keep watch, dog," Orla muttered, laying the bike down on the verge and rummaging in her bag for Uncle Valentine's binoculars. Swivelling the focus ring she zoomed in on the GasFrac compound, counting the yellow brutes. Dave looked on approvingly as she wrote the details in her notebook. She was learning.

Then he let out a low warning growl. A car coming up the hill from the village was slowing down. Dave scanned the target: a male driver and a female passenger. Civilians, early seventies. Low risk.

The car stopped alongside them. It was so old that the bodywork had rotted away, leaving holes that had been filled with concrete. The driver, a gentle-looking man with fluffy white sideburns and a bright red face, forced his fingers through the gap at the top of the window, then, with some effort, pushed it low enough that he could peer out.

"How do?" he called. "Are you lost?"

59

"Good morning," said Orla. "I'm just looking at all those yellow diggers."

"They'll be moving in next Monday," said the lady in the passenger seat. She was wearing big black glasses and had a voice like a pirate. "And about time too."

About time? thought Orla. "Isn't there anything you can do to stop them?" she asked.

The old man shifted in his seat to give Orla a deeply suspicious look, as though she'd asked for a match while standing next to a haystack with a bucket of petrol.

"Why would anyone want to do anything to stop them?" he replied.

"Because what they're doing is wrong," said Orla.

The old lady in the dark glasses shook her head sadly.

"You should mind your own business," she snapped as the concrete car rolled away. "This is the best thing that's..."

Orla didn't catch the rest.

"Hmm," she mused. She lifted the bike, then Dave, dropping him into the basket. "Let's see what they say in the village."

Dave made himself comfortable, looking forward to a gentle and controlled descent into Haddenham St Taylan.

Moments later, his gritted teeth were speckled with flies and his ears were trailing like streamers as Orla hurtled down the hill at breakneck speed. Dave snatched a glimpse of her over his shoulder, her red hair streaming like flames from a doomed aeroplane. He looked to the front again, squinting into the headwind, the verge just a blur and the road getting steeper and steeper as it sucked them towards a ninety-degree right-hand bend in the middle of the village.

Dave looked back at Orla. She'd seen the bend, right?

Three magpies swept in from the left. Dave gave them the evil eye, then glanced at Orla again. Surely she'd seen the bend?

Orla had indeed seen the bend and was now really, really wishing that she'd swallowed her pride and let Uncle Valentine check the brakes. Because, she had just realized, they didn't work. Disaster was now five seconds away. Dead ahead, three seconds away, was the Haddenham St Taylan post office with a yellow motorbike parked outside. Next to it, a privet hedge.

"Adopt the crash position, dog," she cried. "We're going in."

The bike hurtled into the hedge and might have made it clean through had it not been for a stubborn root that trapped the front wheel and sent the pair airborne. Dave had already devised an emergency response, landing on his feet and rolling fast to the side as the bike came crashing down.

Orla landed on her back in a rose bed and wailed. The peck on her cheek had reopened and there was blood on her chin. But as Dave dashed across to check her for further injuries, he realized she wasn't sobbing at all. She was laughing her socks off. He licked the wound on her cheek, happy in spite of himself to see her back in action.

"Excuse me?"

They both looked up. A stern-looking woman in a long dress was staring at them, her hands on her hips.

Orla put on her serious face. She struggled into a sitting position, rubbing her elbow with one hand and wiping her cheek with the other.

"Hello," she said. "We've just had a bike accident. Brakes failed. I'm sorry." She climbed out of the flower bed, brushing the twigs off her sleeves. Then she noticed the broken rose bushes.

"Oh no," she gasped. "I'm so sorry; I can pay for the damage." That wasn't quite true, but she'd find a way.

The woman looked unimpressed, and unsympathetic. "This is post office property," she said, "and I'm the postmistress." She had very short hair and very red lipstick, like a nun on her day off. Orla couldn't help but notice that, apart from the roses, her garden consisted mostly of herbs.

Rare and unusual ones.

"Are you injured?" snapped the postmistress.

Orla's elbows were grazed and her hip hurt, but it was no biggie. "I'm fine," she said.

"You've cut your face," observed the postmistress.

"That was yesterday," said Orla. "A magpie did it." She stepped out of the rose bed and grabbed a handful of yarrow to stop the bleeding. "Better now." She smiled, watching for a reaction. The postmistress gave nothing away, but Orla had a feeling about her.

The postmistress looked at the bicycle. "There's a retired mechanic living at number forty-eight. His name's Ray, and if you ask him nicely, he'll fix your brakes." She glanced sadly at her roses. "I don't know why I bother. Every year it's the same. Last Easter, a sidecar came off a motorcycle and through the hedge. It destroyed my greenhouse. Then there was a camper van in June; and the summer before, a family of four from Germany. It's simply unbearable."

As Orla tried to remove the bike from the carnage of the flower bed without causing more damage, she saw the postmistress throwing a disapproving glance at the gwelen.

Orla sucked a skinned knuckle. "Was it Uncle Valentine's sidecar that destroyed your greenhouse, by any chance?"

"I refuse to discuss that maniac," sniffed the postmistress. Dave paced around her. He could smell something horribly familiar. She threw him a look like a dagger.

This was awkward, thought Orla, extending her hand. "Orla Perry, pleased to meet you. I'm up from London for a holiday. This is Dave."

The lady glanced at Orla's hand and decided against shaking it. "Elizabeth Edwards," she said slowly. "I've heard of you, and I've heard about your dog. I find his loyalty puzzling. All the books say they can't abide the likes of us."

Orla smiled. She'd crashed into a witch's garden – and where better to start her investigation?

"Don't worry about Dave," she said, shielding her mouth so the Jack Russell couldn't see. "He's part cat," she whispered. "Can we talk?"

CHAPTER 5

"Wait here," ordered the postmistress. She shut the back door, locked it and disappeared from view.

Orla waited for her to return, noticing the chalk patterns on the step – a series of interconnected figures of eight – and piles of the magical protection rocks called hag stones on either side of the door. She peered through the glass. Where had the postmistress gone? Should she knock, or give her more time? She glanced at Dave.

"What do you reckon? Is it a trap?" she whispered.

The key turned in the lock.

"Sorry to have kept you waiting," said the postmistress. She didn't look very sorry. "You can come in, but leave the dog outside."

"He'll behave himself," promised Orla.

"I don't care," said Elizabeth Edwards. "This is a post office, and if there's one species dogs hate more than witches, it's Royal Mail employees, so leave him outside and come in."

"Sorry, Dave," sighed Orla.

Dave weed against a flowerpot and shrugged. He was happy to let them chat while he got on with the serious business of working out why magpies had somehow been involved in everything that had gone wrong on this mission.

"Come into the light," ordered the postmistress. "Look up. You've got something stuck in your forehead."

"Ouch," yelped Orla.

"All better now," said the postmistress. A rose thorn like a shark's fin lay in her palm, a drop of blood on its tip. "These can be nasty," she observed. "Hold those yarrow leaves against the wound." She squirted sanitizing gel onto her hands. "Now, what exactly are you doing here?"

Her shop seemed to have been last stocked in 1934. There were balls of string and rolls of brown paper. Cardboard tags with tails of twine. Racks of pens, packs of pencils, bottles of ink and stacks of stationery were carefully arranged on wooden shelves that smelled of polish next to a revolving stand of faded postcards showing churches and windmills and fat seals on blurry beaches. There were boxes of second-hand books, a garland of dried rowan that tourists would think was a flower arrangement rather than a defensive charm, and a photocopier with a sign saying *Out of order*.

"I'm on holiday," said Orla. She pointed at the photocopier. "Uncle Valentine could fix that."

"I've already asked you not to mention him," snapped Elizabeth Edwards.

Orla shrugged, then spotted the cat. A yellow-eyed ginger tom with an arched back and sharp teeth stood on a shelf above the counter. He was definitely dead.

"Who's that?" she asked.

"That's Vinegar Tom," sniffed the postmistress. "My familiar. But you haven't come here to discuss him. Who sent you?"

"My mum," said Orla. "She's gone on a course so we were sent here for the holidays."

Elizabeth Edwards looked alarmed. "I thought it was..." She stopped herself. "I mean to say: how many of you are there?"

"My two brothers and me. Can we talk about Anna's Wood?"

"Nothing to talk about. Especially if you're entertaining some childish fantasy about saving it."

A single ray of sunlight lit up the shop, dust dancing in the beam like fairies.

"But we can't let GasFrac bulldoze it," argued Orla. "What will happen to the birds?"

"There is no *we*, Orla Perry. There are outsiders like you and there are locals like us. And the locals all agree that the GasFrac project is a good thing for the community."

"But why should wildlife die for the sake of a gas pipeline?"

The postmistress opened her glasses case, polished her spectacles, perched them on her nose and fixed Orla with a fierce stare. "Tourists always want quaint villages like this to stay the same but we deserve progress as much as any city dweller. GasFrac will bring jobs and prosperity. They'll give us a country park with parking for three hundred cars and an interpretation centre, and they'll build us a new shopping centre in Hunstanton. They've promised to plant twenty trees for every one they chop down and the wildlife will find somewhere else to live, just like it always does. Everybody wins."

Orla shook her head. "You don't believe that."

The postmistress gave Orla a long, hard look. "Are we done here?"

Orla leaned on the counter. "Can I ask you a question?"

"No. I have customers to serve."

Orla looked around. The door was still locked and the shop was still empty. "Is the wood magic?" she asked.

"Stupid question," said the postmistress. "Off you go."

"It should be magic," insisted Orla. "Don't you think?"

The postmistress swept out from behind the counter, strode across the shop and peeked out at the village through the blinds. She turned to Orla. "Enchanted woods belong in fairy tales. Not in real life."

"So where do you get your sprowl from?"

The postmistress made a face as though she'd been asked an especially inappropriate question. "Where does anyone collect sprowl?" she replied. "In hedgerows, where streams meet, from flint beds and graveyards. Don't you know that it's rude to ask a practitioner to reveal her sources?"

"Sorry," said Orla, not sorry at all. "Can I ask one more question?"

"No."

"Didn't anybody oppose GasFrac?"

"There's always somebody ready to oppose anything," muttered the postmistress. "Outsiders, mostly, like you. Interfering in other people's lives to put meaning into theirs. They got together with the local tree-huggers and arranged a protest campaign, but they soon came to their senses."

"Are the local tree-huggers still here?" asked Orla.

The postmistress put her hands on her hips and looked at Orla the same way her head teacher did when there'd been yet another misunderstanding of school rules.

"They're still here, but they've decided to stop hugging the trees in Anna's Wood. They've seen the benefits and you won't change their minds."

"I can try."

"You are an extremely irritating girl," sighed the postmistress. She stared at Orla, as though making up her mind. Then she pointed west. "Jemima Water-Mills. Former journalist from London and head of the Save Anna's Wood campaign until it folded. She's now a lifestyle influencer, whatever that is. She lives in Burnham Down – the village next door – at the bottom end of Staithe Street. Get Ray to fix your brakes, then go and bother her. I guarantee she will put you off this stupid idea and then you can get on and enjoy your holiday." She took a step closer to Orla. "No good will come of meddling. No good at all."

Dave wandered alongside Orla as she pushed her broken bike along Haddenham St Taylan's empty high street. Grand and shabby houses stood side by side, and all had the same poster in their windows. It showed a grinning family with dazzling teeth emerging excitedly from a shopping centre, weighed down with designer carrier bags. Above their heads was the message *Believe in the Power of Dreams*; below their feet, *GasFrac*.

"Not much resistance here," muttered Orla.

She came to number forty-eight: a dark and overgrown cottage that looked abandoned. It too had a *Believe in the Power of Dreams* poster in the window, and as Orla raised her hand to knock at the peeling grey front door, it opened. A very tall old man with slicked-back black hair, black rings around his eyes and skin that matched the door peered out.

"No, it's not for sale," he growled. "Don't care how much you're offering."

"Pardon?" said Orla.

"The house is not for sale," he repeated. "You tourists come knocking on my door from Easter to All Hallows, always asking the same question. I should put a sign up saying not for sale."

"Are you Ray?" asked Orla.

"Yes." The man nodded. He had a kind face, from the little Orla could see of it.

"I can't afford to buy your house," she said. "But Elizabeth Edwards at the post office said you could probably fix my bike."

"Maybe," replied Ray. "Who are you?"

"I'm Orla Perry and this is Dave," said Orla. "I'm staying at Sicow's Creek with my uncle."

"Valentine Perry?" asked Ray. "He's a good man. Was, anyway. What's wrong with your bicycle?"

"It's the brakes," said Orla.

Dave pushed his nose into the doorway. There were an awful lot of weird smells in that house.

"Oh," said Ray. "Take it around the side to the workshop."

Orla pushed the bike through a garden that looked like a scrapyard and waited for Ray. Two old cars sat on rat-gnawed tyres and a huge ship's anchor was propped up on a pile of rusty girders. Wild buddleia had grown through an old washing machine, turning it, thought Orla, into a work of art, and a plaster statue of a one-armed saint stood on an oil drum. There was a click as another grey door opened and a hand beckoned.

"Give me the bike and wait outside," ordered Ray. "It's dangerous in here."

The clink of spanners and the squeak of rusty nuts came from within as Orla searched Ray's garden for clues. "I heard the bulldozers are going in next Monday," she called.

"Yes," said Ray. "This bike is in a terrible state."

"They'll be smashing down Anna's Wood. Don't you think that's a shame?"

"You need new tyres and that chain replaced," continued Ray. "Tell your uncle."

Dave was sniffing a wooden box full of rusty tins and coils of wire.

"Can't you stop them?"

Ray was silent.

Dave pushed a tin bucket with his nose, surprising a large brown rat. Dave gave it a look that said *prepare to meet thy maker*. The rat returned a look saying *don't kid yourself, fat boy*, and before Dave could react, shot through a hole in the workshop wall.

The bike emerged from the workshop, front wheel first. Ray stayed inside, almost invisible in the gloom. It was as though he were scared that daylight would turn him to dust.

"Blooming great rat just ran through here," he muttered.

"Why don't you care about the wood?" asked Orla.

Ray stood in the shadows with just the tip of his nose exposed to the late morning sunshine.

"It's not about the gas," Orla persisted. "A magpie showed me."

"Did he indeed?"

"She," corrected Orla.

Ray looked at the cracked concrete floor wearily. "The truth about that wood lies below the surface, but not as far down as the bedrock. The problem is that bad things happen to those who speak the truth. Best to keep quiet."

"You can trust me," said Orla. "I promise."

"No, I can't," he growled, "and I won't open my door to you again. There's no charge for the repair. Just two bits of advice. Don't go digging around in Anna's Wood; but if you do, do not for pity's sake get caught. Now go."

Feeling uneasy, Orla pedalled two miles west to the tiny village of Burnham Down, where she found Staithe Street just past the church. It was a street of modest, almost

73

identical Victorian cottages, all displaying the GasFrac poster. Then she came to the last in the row: a headache-inducing explosion of chintz, festooned with bunting, Chinese lanterns and smoke-blackened jars with tea lights in them. A big sign announced that this was *The GENUINE Norfolk Cottage Garden*. A smaller one said *Photographs welcome in signposted areas only – please tag #NorfolkCottageGarden*. An even smaller one said *No dogs* but Orla pretended not to see it. Clipping Dave onto his lead, she pushed open the lilac-painted gate and stepped into the garden.

"Hello?" she called. "I'm Orla Perry. Can I come in?"

A big woman in a long flowery dress with a scarf wrapped around her head popped up from behind a bush.

"Welcome to hashtag Norfolk Cottage Garden dot com." She beamed. "I know what you're thinking. Is this the actual Jemima Water-Mills? Well, yes, it is. Amazing, huh?" Then she saw Dave and frowned. "No dogs, thank you."

"But he's my support animal," said Orla. "And if I leave him outside, he might be stolen."

Jemima Water-Mills sighed, then smiled. She seemed much nicer than Elizabeth Edwards. "Well, seeing as it's quiet today, I can make an exception as long as he doesn't wee anywhere."

Orla could never guarantee that, but she nodded anyway. "I just want to ask a few questions," she began.

"Of course," said Jemima. "And I suppose you'd like a selfie with me?"

"Not really," said Orla.

"Don't be silly," giggled Jemima. "Come on, I'll give you the exclusive VIP tour."

It was a beautiful garden, but as Orla followed Jemima with Dave at her side, she wondered if this was how Hansel and Gretel must have felt as they were led astray by the wicked witch.

"Everything is grown from organic seed," said Jemima proudly. "I collect most of it myself or trade it among friends. We're almost totally cashless in the community, doing everything by barter. I only use local manure and seaweed as fertilizer and all the rainwater is recycled. I'm guessing you follow me on SplishSplash?"

"No," said Orla.

"YouBook?"

"No."

"Binkywinkygram?"

Orla shrugged. "I don't have a mobile."

Jemima Water-Mills looked horrified, but then her smile returned. "I've got nearly two hundred thousand followers, you know. Norfolk Cottage Garden is the account."

Orla hung back for a moment, admiring the red tulips, the deep blue irises and the happy yellow polyanthus. These were flowers chosen for prettiness, not usefulness. Jemima Water-Mills, realized Orla, was no witch. At least, not the kind she was used to.

"Are you a hashtag gardener?" asked Jemima.

"I'm not," said Orla. "But I'd hashtag like to be one day."

"Good for you." Jemima smiled. "I love your necklace, by the way. Did you make it yourself?"

Orla's hand flew self-consciously to the star around her neck. "No," she said. "I bought it."

"Very rustic." Jemima nodded. "Would you like to buy a copy of my book?"

"No," said Orla. "I'd like to know why you're not fighting GasFrac."

Jemima slapped a hand over her mouth. "Oh," she said. "What did you say your name was?"

"I'm Orla Perry, and I want to know why you stopped fighting for Anna's Wood, please."

Jemima sighed. "How old are you, dear?"

"I'm thirteen." Orla frowned. She was beginning to think she preferred the postmistress.

"Well, come and sit down, young lady," said Jemima. She led Orla up the garden path to a table and four chairs in the shade of a low and twisted apple tree. "Sit, please," she invited, but Orla remained standing. Jemima was pretending to be nice, but it wasn't working.

"Why didn't you fight GasFrac? You've got two hundred thousand followers."

"At first we thought we should fight them because, well, nature is so important, obviously, but we didn't know the facts." Jemima shrugged. "GasFrac showed us that not all invasions are bad. Sometimes resistance is not only silly but just plain wrong."

"How can saving an ancient woodland be just plain wrong?" asked Orla. "Did GasFrac pay you?"

"GasFrac has donated a considerable sum to local environmental causes," admitted Jemima, "and – hashtag full disclosure – they've supported Norfolk Cottage Garden with a generous sponsorship deal through their environmental goals scheme. And because we've all decided to work with GasFrac and truly believe in the power of dreams, that silly Save Anna's Wood campaign has been officially closed down."

Orla took a deep breath. Keep calm, she told herself. Control the anger. Resist the urge to be rude. "So, basically, they offered money to keep quiet and you took it?" she said.

Jemima smiled again, blinking as though the sunshine was a spotlight and she was receiving an award. "Life

77

seems so simple when you're only thirteen, Orla. I think the idea that you can achieve anything is wonderful, but as you grow up you begin to realize that sometimes you have to compromise – stop fighting for the best solution and choose instead the least worst option."

As Dave took a wee up the apple tree, Orla could feel a vein beginning to throb in her head. "Is letting GasFrac destroy an ancient wood and the most beautiful chalk stream in Norfolk really the least worst option? What could actually be worse than that?"

Jemima beamed. "I love your feistiness, Orla. I love the way you're willing to fight for a better world, and I can see that you too believe in the power of dreams. I know everybody has the same dreams these days, but once upon a time they were like snowflakes: every one different and impossible to recreate."

"Do people have the same dreams?" asked Orla. "Mine are pretty weird."

Jemima smiled. "They won't be for long. But believing in the power of dreams is good. This beautiful garden is built on dreams. Through sheer hard work and determination, I became the thirty-fourth highest rated British organic gardening account on SelfieObsession."

Suddenly her smile disappeared, like the sun slipping behind a black cloud.

"But I learned something along the way, young lady. To survive in this world, you should only pick the battles you can win. And I also learned that if you go meddling in other people's business, you can get badly hurt."

CHAPTER 6

"Uh-oh," muttered Tom as Orla and Dave burst into Sicow's Creek like an irritated SWAT team. "Here comes trouble."

He watched as his sister snatched Dave's water bowl from the kitchen floor, filled it, poured herself a glass and downed it in three angry gulps.

"We've got a problem," she growled.

"Think I'll just, um, pop to my room," said Tom. He carefully placed a tiny railway carriage into the shoebox on the table and pushed back his chair.

"Stay where you are," barked Orla, unclipping Dave's harness. "Where's Richard?"

"Out there," said Tom meekly, nodding towards the window. "He was helping UV launch the mussel flat."

For a few moments, the only sound was Dave thirstily lapping up his water. Then the back door opened. Richard's eyes flicked from Orla to Tom then back to Orla.

"Who died?" he asked.

"We need to talk about Anna's Wood," announced Orla.

Tom groaned. "Please don't tell me it's cursed."

"Not cursed. Doomed. Unless we can do something."

"Why us?" said Richard. He opened the fridge and pulled out a can of something unrecognizable. "It's not our wood. Not our battle. It's up to the locals."

"The locals have given up," said Orla. "They've been brainwashed or paid off – or both. I met the postmistress today. She's a witch. She as much as admitted it, and she said the GasFrac project was a good thing because of a country park and a shopping centre. Then I met this weird man called Ray who said bad things happened to those who spoke the truth, and a creepy influencer called Jemima Water-Mills who was head of the Save Anna's Wood campaign until GasFrac paid her to keep quiet. Earlier some old people said it was about time the diggers went into the wood. And everyone – I mean *everyone* – has posters in their windows showing some lame family out shopping and believing in the power of dreams."

"Did you meet anyone who didn't believe in the power of dreams?" asked Richard. He popped the can, took a tentative sip and nodded in approval.

Orla shook her head.

"So since one hundred per cent of those you surveyed said they didn't care about the wood, why should we?"

"Because it's a special place."

"More special than any other wood?" asked Tom.

Orla nodded. "Tons more special."

"Why?"

Orla braced herself. Her brothers weren't going to like what was coming next.

"I went there last night," she said. "In a dream. I saw terrible things."

Richard rolled his eyes. "Like most dreams, it would have been inspired by events and conversations of the previous day when, as I recall, you were pecked by a one-footed magpie and fed a load of rural hocus-pocus."

"No," protested Orla. "This was more than a dream. It was the vision of the future that Uncle Valentine was talking about." She knew exactly how crazy this sounded, but she ploughed on. "The magpie – I think she wanted me to see what would happen to the birds if the wood was destroyed."

"What does happen to them?" asked Tom.

"They all die. I saw it and it was horrible." She fixed her brothers with a long, hard stare. "I can't let that happen. Will you help me stop GasFrac?"

Richard flopped into a chair in sudden despair. Tom put his head in his hands and groaned. Dave crept away and hid behind the sofa.

"Why can't we just have a normal holiday like normal kids?" wailed Tom. "Why is there always some drama?"

"I'm sorry," said Orla. "But there's something very, very weird going on in Anna's Wood."

"The only weird stuff is in your head," said Richard. "You promised there'd be no witchcraft on this holiday and, oh look, it's only day two and it's like *The Wizard of Oz* in here."

Orla persisted. "It's inexplicable – like a patch of primeval forest that has somehow survived in the farmland. It doesn't belong here. Come and see for yourself. Tom?"

Tom pretended to give the idea some consideration while he opened a bag of smoky bacon crisps. "No thanks," he said eventually.

Orla let out a growl of frustration. "Can't you see that this doesn't add up? Old people hate change, but those I met are all for it. People who like organic gardening should be opposed to fracking, and yet Jemima Water-Mills just caved in when they offered her money; and the postmistress is a witch, and our duty as witches..."

Richard raised an eyebrow. Tom stopped crunching crisps.

"*Their* duty as witches, I mean, is to protect nature above all. But everyone is on GasFrac's side."

Richard put his can on the table, rubbed his eyes with his fists and took a deep breath. "Let me explain," he said.

"Trees are a natural resource. We cut them down for fuel or for building and new ones take their place. Gas is a natural resource too. The energy it provides powers our laptops, our schools and our hospitals, and when the gas is gone the site will probably be returned to nature. In the meantime, the locals get jobs, a country park and a shopping centre. What's wrong with that?"

Orla's jaw dropped. "Are you serious?" She looked from Richard to Tom.

"Sorry," Tom said. He glanced down sheepishly.

"I'm speechless," spluttered Orla, striding across the kitchen. "Utterly speechless. I'm going to lie down."

She grabbed her gwelen and paused at the foot of the stairs. "Dog?" she yelled. "Come on."

Dave slipped deeper into the murk behind the sofa. With her in that mood? No chance.

She reappeared two hours later as Uncle Valentine and the boys were preparing dinner.

"Where are you off to?" asked the old man. "There's crumble needs baking and I've got to check my nets. And can you ask your dog not to sit on the windowsill like a Persian cat?"

"I need some air," said Orla abruptly. "Richard can bake the crumble."

"You're up to no good," said Tom, pointing an accusing carrot.

"I am not," she replied, unconvincingly. "Come on, dog. Let's go."

Dave leapt from his duck-watching position and ambled over to escort her. The door clicked as they went out into the marsh, following the footpath back towards the road.

When she was sure she couldn't be seen, she pulled Richard's iPhone from her pocket. She logged in using the complicated passcode Richard thought no one knew, and then walked until she found a spot with a signal. It was weak, but it would do. She carefully tapped in a number she had memorized at the end of last summer, let it ring three times, then hung up, counted to sixty and dialled again. This time she let it ring twice, hung up, counted to thirty and dialled yet again. It was answered on the first ring.

"What's the problem?"

"We need to talk," said Orla.

"Not on the phone."

"But we're encrypted."

"Not very well. I can see your location. I'll come to you."

"There's really no need," said Orla.

"There is, otherwise you wouldn't have called this number. Destroy the phone. I'll be there tomorrow."

The line went dead. Orla looked at the phone. Richard's

entire life was in her hand. She couldn't destroy it, no matter how satisfying it might be.

She walked back from the road, past the house and onto the crooked wooden dock on Sicow's Creek. Night was falling, the marsh had crept under a blanket of mist and the low yellow crescent moon had been outshone by the arc lights from the GasFrac compound. Orla sat on the end of the jetty, legs swinging and her stomach full of anguish. Dave sat behind her and licked his bum.

Whichever way she looked at Anna's Wood, it made no sense. It was exactly the sort of place that should have been protected from GasFrac by an army of conservationists, scientists, schoolkids, journalists and celebrities, and yet it seemed as though they'd all given up without a fight.

Last night's dream was of nature left to die for profit – to make rich people richer. It was still vivid in her head, and she knew it wasn't really a dream. She'd been kissed by a one-footed magpie and granted a vision of a future made of concrete and barbed wire. Was she supposed to just accept it?

"Getting enough air?" called Uncle Valentine, emerging from the mist like the ferryman on the Styx. "Aren't you cold?"

He was standing on the stern of the mussel flat – a long, low boat that he propelled with a pole. Orla shook her head and watched as he slid alongside the dock.

"Do you believe in the power of dreams, Uncle Valentine?"

The old man grunted. "That's the GasFrac line."

"Didn't any of you dream about saving Anna's Wood?" she asked.

Uncle Valentine tied the bowline to the dock, lifted a rattling net of mussels out of the flat and lowered it into the water. Then he patted Dave on the head and sat down next to Orla, groaning in the way that old people do.

"We did," he said. "And it was more than dreams. We fought for it tooth and nail. Posters, marches, sit-ins – the whole protest package. We had activists up from London and Bristol, and that Jemima Water-Mills was on TV once a week. Then there was that other bloke off the telly. Lives in a big manor house over Watlington way. Thinks he's terribly clever. Not clever enough, as it turned out."

"So why did you give up?"

Uncle Valentine rubbed his beard and stared across the marsh; the arc lights reflected in his eyes.

"I can't tell you, Orla, because I don't know. But one by one they came to the conclusion that chopping the wood down and covering it in concrete in return for a shopping centre and a country park was a good idea. I have no idea why. None of them talk to me any more."

He swung his legs like Orla. "Not that I mind much."

Orla looked at him, his salt-cured face half hidden beneath that piratical red beard.

"Do you think there's still time?" she asked.

"Time for what?"

"Time to save Anna's Wood."

Uncle Valentine gazed across the mist that swirled like mustard gas to where the GasFrac lights defied the night. Then he turned to Orla.

"You know what? I gave your brother Richard an old telly to fix and Thomas a broken train set. Couldn't think of a project for you because I don't know what girls do, but now you've gone and found a project for yourself." Orla heard his bones creak as he stood up. "I can't see you succeeding, but by crikey, girl, it's worth a try. Cat's never dead till it's buried."

Orla started. "Where did you hear that?"

Uncle Valentine shrugged. "It's just something some people say."

Except it wasn't. Orla knew it was usually something only a witch would say, but there was no need to go into that now.

"I met Jemima Water-Mills today," she said as they walked back to the house.

"Sorry to hear that. Did she make you buy a book?"

Orla shook her head. "I met the postmistress too."

Uncle Valentine nodded. "Liz the Whizz."

"She speaks very highly of you."

Uncle Valentine laughed. "I sincerely doubt that."

"Do you know her?"

Something wistful flickered across her uncle's face. "You've seen that yellow Honda she rides? I rebuilt it for her."

Orla noticed the spark in his eyes.

"Did you meet anyone else?" he asked.

"A shy man called Ray."

"Crepuscular Ray. You never see him out in daylight."

"Wow. Well, he said my bike needs new tyres and a chain and told me not to get caught in Anna's Wood. And I met an old man in a concrete car with a lady in dark glasses."

"Charlie Cement Wings and the Moon Queen," said Uncle Valentine. "She gathers cockles by the light of the moon. Blind as a bat by day, but she knows the tides. But not everyone round these parts is like the people you met today. We've got some weird folk here too."

CHAPTER 7

It was just after 6.30 a.m. on the last day before the madness began – the final sunlit hour of relative normality at Sicow's Creek. Orla was sitting on the top step with the binoculars, watching a pair of bar-tailed godwits probing the tidal mud for breakfast with their long beaks. Dave was at her feet, napping in the low sunshine, and Richard and Uncle Valentine were at the kitchen table, tinkering with the TV. Tom had been sent to the workshop to fetch a pair of needle-nose pliers. He'd gone slowly – still in a state of shock at being forced to get up so early – but he came back at full speed.

"We've got company," he called, stamping up the steps past Orla to deliver the pliers.

Uncle Valentine looked up from a circuit board. "Probably a lost hiker."

Tom shook his head. "Not a hiker." He grabbed the binoculars from Orla and ran back down the steps.

"Hey!" she called, but Tom ignored her.

"She's wearing weird clothes and she's carrying a suitcase," he said. "She looks like a time traveller."

"Why don't you save her the effort of walking all the way out here by going to meet her and politely informing her that Sicow's Creek is not an Airbnb?" suggested Uncle Valentine.

"Cos she's already here," said Tom.

A short girl with flicked black hair and dark eyes came around the side of the house. She was wearing a red turtleneck, a knee-length brown skirt and long suede boots. She had a leather satchel over her shoulder and her suitcase, like her look, was pure 1970s.

"Good morning," she said.

Orla smiled, rising to her feet. "Morning. Good to see you."

Richard came to the doorway. His jaw dropped.

"Oh my God," he exclaimed. "Raven?"

The girl shook her head. "The name's Meadows," she said. "Misty Meadows."

"Really?" asked Orla dubiously. She'd met this girl last summer, sleeping rough on a Cornish clifftop. They'd started out as enemies and become friends, but that person had been a goth called Raven.

The newcomer nodded. "That's right. Misty Meadows, investigative reporter."

"Investigative reporter?" asked Tom, rather sceptically.

Uncle Valentine looked at the suitcase. "You planning on staying long, Miss Meadows?"

"Just until the job is done."

"What job?" asked Richard.

"She's come to help us save the wood," announced Orla. "And she's just in time for breakfast."

After they'd eaten, Orla spread an Admiralty chart dated 1938 across the kitchen table. She showed Raven/Misty the GasFrac compound, Haddenham St Taylan and the Swallow Valley. Then she pointed at a whirl of contours blotting the river like a fingerprint.

"Anna's Wood," she said.

"Weird topography," observed Misty. She picked up the yellow teacup and looked inside. "Nice stones."

"A magpie brings them," said Orla matter-of-factly. "She brought me the blue one yesterday and the red one today."

"You have a strange relationship with animals," noted Misty. "But pretty pebbles won't stop bulldozers. We need to make a plan. Take a seat, kids. And you, Mr Perry. Chop-chop."

"Misty isn't a name," sniffed Richard, dragging another chair to the table. "It's a weather forecast."

"Ha ha," said Misty.

"To be fair, Raven wasn't really a name either," added Tom. "Unless you were a bird of unusual intelligence."

"Raven is gone," said Misty. "Flown away. And if anyone asks, you never knew her." She gave Dave a curious look. "Has Dave put on weight since last summer?"

"Totally let himself go," said Tom. "Too many pies."

Unbelievable, thought Dave.

"Hey," warned Orla, lifting him onto her lap. "He's still head of household security. Be nice."

Misty pulled a reporter's notebook and a chewed biro from her satchel.

"Do you actually work for a newspaper?" asked Tom curiously.

"I will when I've written this story. The first question a good reporter asks is always who's the bad guy?"

"No," said Richard. "The first question is what are you doing here?"

"I called her," said Orla. "On your phone."

Richard began to splutter but Misty waved his concern away. "I heard you needed help so I caught the last train to London, slept at King's Cross and jumped the mail train to King's Lynn."

"That's only about halfway," noted Richard. "How did you get to Psycho's Creek?"

"On a potato truck," shrugged Misty. "The driver was called Italian Barry."

"I know him," nodded Uncle Valentine. "He's not really Italian."

"Good to know," said Misty, "but I didn't come here to talk about Barry. I have my own theory about what's really happening here but I need to hear it from you. Who's the bad guy?"

"That'll be GasFrac," said Uncle Valentine. "It's an energy company owned by some fellow called Thorn." He pointed out of the kitchen window to where a skein of geese was flying in arrow formation across the marsh. "They're camped out over yonder."

"They're a fracking company," added Richard. "They extract oil and natural gas from—"

"I know what a fracking company does, thanks," Misty interrupted impatiently. "What's underneath the wood?"

"Enough natural gas to power four cities for five years, they reckon," said Uncle Valentine. "The plan is to pipe it through a refinery and onto gas carriers at a floating dock in the bay."

Misty scribbled in her notebook. "Who gave GasFrac permission to move into the wood?"

"The district council in Cromer," said Uncle Valentine.

94

"So that's where the surveys and the EIAs are," mused Misty.

She seemed to be quite good at investigative journalism, thought Orla.

"What are EIAs?" asked Richard.

"Environmental Impact Assessments," explained Misty. "Companies like GasFrac have to write a report explaining what the environmental effects of their operations will be and what they'll do to repair the damage. If we can get copies, we might find something that's been overlooked, or something that GasFrac forgot to mention."

"Would that stop them?" asked Orla.

Misty shrugged. "Maybe. But it would definitely delay them and buy us time to get a protest movement started."

"We tried that once already," muttered Uncle Valentine.

"And you failed," noted Misty. "This time we'll do it properly. Are we in contact with any concerned locals?"

"No friendly ones," said Orla. She ran through her list, starting with the postmistress and ending with Jemima Water-Mills.

"Hmm," continued Misty, "if we can't count on the law or locals willing to chain themselves to trees, we've got a third option. A secret weapon. An ultimate deterrent."

"Oh yes?" said Uncle Valentine. "What would that be?"

"Witchcraft," announced Misty.

Uncle Valentine looked puzzled. "As it happens, I know a bit about witchcraft," he said, "and it's my understanding that one of the main things you need to make it work is a witch. And you don't have one."

Orla made big no-no eyes at Misty. Tom threw a pencil on the floor to create a diversion. Dave pounced on it and Richard started coughing. Misty didn't notice any of it.

"We've got a witch," she said. "She's sitting right next to you."

Uncle Valentine pushed his chair back, slammed his hands down on the table and spun to look at Orla.

"Are you a witch?" he cried.

Orla made snake eyes at Misty, and gave Uncle Valentine a small smile.

"Er, yes," she confessed. "Sort of. I mean, not seriously. Is that OK?"

Uncle Valentine stared at her, long and hard, then let out a heavy sigh. "I saw that big stick and it crossed my mind. You won't be the first under this roof. Are you any good at it?"

"Not really," said Orla.

"She's brilliant," argued Tom.

"She's totally amazing," agreed Misty. "Isn't she, Richard?"

Richard shrugged. "She's not bad. For a phone thief."

"Do you practise?" asked Uncle Valentine. "Because you should. It's a gift. You can't waste it."

Orla grunted. If being a witch was a gift, she'd have asked for the receipt so she could take it back and get something less troublesome.

Misty looked at her watch: a shiny digital affair from the 1970s. "It's eight fifteen," she said. "Time to get to work. We'll each do what we do best. Richard and I will go to Cromer and find those EIAs and any paperwork to do with GasFrac's application. Tom, you stay here and search the outhouses for anything that could be useful if we have to move to the sabotage phase."

Tom gave a double thumbs up.

"Orla, fetch sprowl. Have you got your gwelen? We need enough sprowl to stop an army."

Orla's heart sank. There wasn't enough sprowl around here to stop a bus.

"Mr Perry?" said Misty. "I need you to—"

Uncle Valentine held his rough old hands in the air. "Hold your horses there, Miss Meadows," he said. "I've got business of my own to attend to. I'll be back at four. You lot make sure you're home before dark."

CHAPTER 8

It was a gorgeous April day of blue skies, fluffy clouds and warm sunshine on the North Norfolk coast. Out on the beaches normal kids were flying kites, building sandcastles and having picnics. Not rushing about on a creaky old bike in search of magical energy. And failing.

Orla sat beneath a roadside oak chewing despondently on a bread sandwich. It had been a cheese sandwich but the cheese had slipped out and Dave had caught it before it hit the ground. He was lying beside her now, keeping watch for magpies while Orla racked her brain for reasons why this seemingly magical countryside had absolutely no sprowl whatsoever.

She'd been to an ancient fort, the meeting of streams, picked twigs from blackthorn hedges and traipsed around churchyards. She'd sought out tumuli – ancient burial grounds – and even hiked across a field to touch her gwelen on an erratic, which was a block of quartz brought from far away by a glacier. But she hadn't found a single drop.

It was inexplicable. Impossible. Sprowl was everywhere, all the time, even if it was in tiny, wisp-like amounts. She'd even found some in Tesco once, and in the maths section of the school library. It was impossible that there was none in Norfolk. Or had she simply lost the skill?

She sat up, picking grass and twigs from her hair, and tapped Dave on the shoulder.

"Let's go, dog," she said. "We need enough sprowl to stop an army, and if we can't find our own, we'll have to borrow some."

Orla knew that the postmistress wouldn't be pleased to see her again, but she'd rather underestimated how unwelcome she was in Haddenham St Taylan. The bell on the door was still tinkling as Elizabeth Edwards swept out from behind the counter, shaking her head angrily, and with a finger across her lips, spun Orla around and pushed her into the street.

She was really quite strong, thought Orla, but as she turned to protest, bolts were shot, locks turned and the post office *Open* sign flipped to *Sorry We're Closed*. As a trio of magpies landed one by one in the tree across the road, she pressed her face against the glass, trying to see past the notices for lost cats, the Anna's Wood Steering Group (*believing in the power of dreams*) and the GasFrac Community Arts programme (*unleashing the power of dreams*) in vain.

Orla looked at Dave. What on earth was going on?

A dusty blind dropped with a clatter. Moments later, it was pulled aside as the postmistress pushed a scrawled message against the glass.

He hears everything.

You have put us all in danger.

Never come here again.

A silver-ringed hand shook the paper, as though trying to throw the words at Orla.

Dave nodded towards the hole in the hedge they'd made yesterday morning.

"Well spotted." Orla nodded with approval as she followed the Jack Russell through the privet.

The postmistress beat her to the back door, throwing her weight against it as she turned the key.

"I need to talk to you," began Orla, but she was silenced by a furious look and a frantic tapping of the lips from the postmistress.

"Well, how can I..." protested Orla, but the postmistress had gone.

"Fine," said Orla. "If you don't come back and talk to me, I'm going to start singing."

It was a serious threat. No one liked to hear Orla Perry sing.

"I'm counting to three," warned Orla. "One."

The magpies cackled.

"Two."

Dave stretched in preparation, performing a perfect downward dog and a tongue-curling yawn.

"Three," called Orla. "Don't say you weren't warned. This one's called 'The Battle Hymn of the Republic'."

She took a deep breath and began singing. It was awful.

"'Mine eyes have seen the glory of the coming of the Lord, He is trampling out the vintage where the grapes of wrath are stored; He has loosed the fateful lightning of His terrible swift sword'" – she could never get the high note right at that bit – "'His truth is marching on', two three four," screeched Orla, waving her gwelen like a giant conductor's baton. "Join in, dog."

And as Orla wailed, "'Glory, glory, hallelujah!'" Dave threw back his head and howled.

It was a terrible din: a tuneless cacophony of tone-deaf caterwauling. Across the village, birds fled and small animals sought cover. The postmistress held out for the first chorus, but, as Orla had predicted, she broke before the beginning of the second verse. The back door flew open and she stood there with a broom in her hand as though preparing for take-off. The other hand was holding a piece of paper.

STOP IT NOW! it said.

Orla held up the fingers of one hand and mouthed, *Five minutes, I promise.*

The postmistress finally realized she had no choice and angrily beckoned her into the shop. It was dark and smelled of fear. Vinegar Tom stared down with yellow glass eyes, his expression even more furious than his mistress's.

The postmistress scribbled on a yellow Post-it note and held it up.

No talking whatsoever.

Orla pulled her notebook and a pencil from her backpack.

I need sprowl, she wrote. She flipped the page and added: *PS Why can't we talk? Is this place bugged?*

The postmistress read the request and scowled. She snatched the book and scribbled: *I knew you'd come back here. Just give up this stupidity.*

Her handwriting was extremely neat, thought Orla. She underlined her previous question: *PS Why can't we talk?*

He hears everything, wrote the postmistress.

Who's he?

The postmistress shook her head. *You need to leave.*

Need sprowl to save birds.

The postmistress underlined her previous comment three times and pointed at the back door.

I've been searching all morning, wrote Orla. *There's nothing. You must have some stored.*

She turned to look around the shop and winced as her backpack knocked a box of biros off the shelf.

Sorry! she wrote, then bent to pick up the spilled pens.

The postmistress scrawled furiously, digging the pen into the notebook like a spade.

You have no idea who you are meddling with.

So tell me! wrote Orla.

Outside, the magpies were chattering like castanets. The postmistress jabbed a finger at the back door. Orla folded her arms and stood her ground.

People will die, scribbled the postmistress. Her handwriting wasn't so neat now.

Seriously???

The postmistress shook her head again.

She really was scared, thought Orla, and while she didn't want to cause distress, right now Elizabeth Edwards was the only person who could help.

The magpies were going crazy as a big black pickup truck rolled to a stop outside the post office. Suddenly the postmistress looked truly terrified. She pointed urgently at the back door.

Orla shook her head. Someone knocked on the door, loud and persistent, like a police officer.

I need to know what's going on here, she wrote. *And I need sprowl. Please.*

Little red circles burned on the postmistress's face. She grabbed the notebook and scrawled:

St Withberga

St Walstan

St Judith

She hesitated, her eyes darting like a trapped bird, then wrote another name.

Kevin D

Orla nodded her thanks. She scanned the list. They're churches, she thought. All except Kevin D. Deconsecrated ones used for witches' rituals. She'd marked them on her map before coming so she could avoid going anywhere near them. Fat chance of that. The knocking came again, louder, and more urgent. But who was Kevin D?

The postmistress grabbed Orla's arm and dragged her around the counter.

A rough voice called, "Miss Edwards? Can you open up, please?"

Orla grabbed the postmistress's arm and leaned close. "Where can I find Kevin?" she hissed.

The woman ripped the front page from the *Lynn News* and thrust it at Orla before pushing her into the back garden and locking the door. Dave let out a warning growl as Orla exited, and she ducked down, creeping to the hole in the hedge as the magpies whirled overhead like enemy drones.

She peeked through the gap at the black pickup truck. Green GasFrac logos were stencilled on the door and the bumper sticker said, unsurprisingly, *Believe in the Power of Dreams*. A walkie-talkie squawked, and Orla could see two men in big black boots and bomber jackets. She could hear the postmistress speaking but couldn't make out any of the words except for "migraine". It was the excuse her mum always used too.

Dave slunk away, his body low to the ground. He'd already scoped out the post office garden for an escape route but he needed to check that the enemy hadn't got it covered before he escorted Orla out of danger.

One of the men was talking into the walkie-talkie, but all Orla heard was "hole in the hedge". Then she saw the boots moving towards the gap. Orla slipped behind the potting shed, noticing the fox spine hanging as a protection against evil intent. She wondered if it worked.

"Happens all the time," she heard the postmistress say. "Cyclists don't see the bend. It's no bother, honestly."

"Better if me and Lee check it out, madam," said one of the goons. "Might be a thief hiding back there."

"In which case," said the postmistress in her haughtiest voice, "it's a matter for the constabulary and not a couple of private security guards."

"Can't hurt to have a look," insisted the other goon. "Get Ace, Trev."

Ace was the German shepherd Orla and Dave had narrowly avoided in the wood. Orla had no desire to meet him again. She looked at Dave. It was now or never.

"This is post office property and I absolutely forbid you to trespass!" shouted Elizabeth Edwards. "I'm going to call the police." Her heels clattered on the pavement and the goon at the gap hesitated for a moment before following her.

"We're only trying to be helpful," said Lee. "We..."

Orla sprinted across the garden. Dave checked she was on his tail, then scrabbled up the six-foot wall like a panther and jumped from the top, landing on all four paws. There was a thud as Orla's gwelen landed beside him. He grabbed it, darted across the lane and cleared the churchyard wall in a single bound. Orla joined him and the pair lay behind the biggest gravestone they could find, chests heaving. As Ace's frustrated barking came from the post office garden, and Dave kept an eye on the three magpies on the tower, Orla read the epitaph on the headstone:

STRANGER, PAUSE ERE YOU PASS BY
AS YOU ARE NOW SO ONCE WAS I
AS I AM NOW YOU SOON WILL BE
PREPARE MY FRIEND THY GOD TO SEE

A chill ran down her spine, and then she spotted more carvings: newly, neatly chiselled on the underside of the window ledges and quite invisible from a standing position.

DAL

It was as though they were only for the dead to read.

She shook her head. This was a minor concern. The big question was the identity of the man capable of striking such terror into the postmistress. Who was *he* who heard everything?

CHAPTER 9

The thought was still buzzing around Orla's head an hour later as she and Dave tramped like lost souls along a muddy track between two bare fields. No trees or hedgerows provided cover, and they both felt vulnerable to attack – especially since the fresh tyre tracks in the mud showed that someone had very recently been this way. Their destination was St Walstan's: a sixth-century church abandoned by Christians for the past four hundred years.

Its ruins stood in a tangle of nettle and bramble: roofless, eyeless and unloved. Or not quite, noted Orla: the white poo and bony pellets on the ancient threshold were evidence that a barn owl lived there, dining on a congregation of rabbits.

Stepping into the rubble-strewn nave, the clouds drifting over broken arches, Orla smiled in grim recognition. This was a place where witches came – a space that had probably been sacred for centuries before Christians built their shrine and was still sacred now they had gone. She let her staff lead her, waiting to feel the comforting heat and the faint tremor of sprowl being absorbed into the blackthorn. But there was nothing here. Nothing but rabbit bones, chisel dust and a fresh carving on the wall:

DAL

It was the same at St Withberga's – an overgrown roadside ruin where broken bottles lay among the fallen tombstones. Orla walked seven times around the broken walls – always in the sinistral, or anticlockwise direction – swishing her staff backwards and forward like a blind man searching for tripwires, but St Withberga's had nothing. Except human footprints in the weeds, and neatly chiselled into the floor:

DAL

What did it mean? Was it a sign for others that the sprowl had been taken, wondered Orla as she pedalled towards St Judith's, the last – and furthest – church on the list. It could be a sign from Christians as a warning to witches. Or was it GasFrac? Were they stealing sprowl to stop witches fighting them? Did energy companies employ experts on witchcraft?

She stopped pedalling and looked at Dave. "Could we be up against a witch, dog? I really, really hope not."

She hid the bike in a hawthorn thicket at the edge of the hamlet of Wissenby and took a narrow, muddy footpath into a beech wood, pausing to pick dried rowan berries from last summer. There was sprowl here. She felt it instantly, but it didn't feel good. Finding sprowl was usually a satisfying feeling, like a cold drink on a hot day, but this sprowl hurt. It made her teeth ache and her fingernails throb. Still, she had no choice but to take it. Hopefully there'd be enough here to stop an army. If not...

She and Dave walked further into the wood.

"Oh my God," gasped Orla.

They'd found St Judith's. It was a magnificent ruin, begun by humans but taken over by nature and still a work in progress. The nave stood fifty feet high and open to the sky, the flint and mortar held together by a mesh of ivy. A single beech grew where the altar would have been and an oak had sent a cradling arm through an arched window. The floor was made of fallen leaves; the graveyard was a garden of moss.

There was a huge amount of stored sprowl hidden here. Orla could sense it in her bones – literally; it felt like her jaw was in an engineer's vice and her legs were being kicked by donkeys. In her left hand the gwelen burned like hot iron, but she refused to turn back. The plaster on the walls was cracked and water stained, but the frescoes were still visible: God and the Devil side by side above the altar. Except it wasn't the Devil and this was no representation of good and evil. The horned one was Bucca Dhu, the old God, alongside the new God. Shoulder to shoulder they were here as equals. One and the same.

Dave darted ahead, sniffing the bat droppings, peering under roots, peeing against trees.

"Seek it out," called Orla. She was always impressed by Dave's mission focus, but her gwelen would find the sprowl first. She swept the stick back and forth, switching hands when it got too hot and scanning the walls and the floor for new carvings. There were none.

Suddenly Dave's tail went into overdrive, wagging back and forth like high-speed windscreen wipers. He let out a gruff woof, then ran in a tight circle before returning to the spot and pawing at the floor. Orla took a deep breath and walked forward, eyes focused on Dave rather than the pain shooting up and down her back. He was scratching at a small slab, telling her there was something buried beneath.

So much for the gwelen beating the dog to the treasure.

"Good boy," she whispered.

She tapped the slab with her staff and it was snatched from her hand as though she'd touched a super magnet.

It stood there, upright and quivering, balanced on its tip upon the stone.

"Whoa," gasped Orla. She looked at Dave. "I've never seen that before."

Dave growled. He didn't understand it, and he rarely liked what he couldn't understand.

Orla crouched down, pulling her penknife from her backpack. After scraping the dirt from the crevices around the slab, she used a screwdriver borrowed from Uncle Valentine's workshop to lever it up. In the cavity beneath was a bundle wrapped in brown sackcloth and tied with red twine.

Orla grinned. "We've struck gold, dog." She pulled out her notebook and pencil and made a quick sketch of the bundle's exact position before removing it from its hiding place, replacing the slab and spreading leaves back on top. She picked up the package like an archaeologist handling a priceless treasure.

"Wonder what's inside?" she said, one eye shut against the crazy throbbing in her head and biting her lip to offset the stabbing in her bones. As she fumbled with the string, Dave danced from one paw to the other, growling with increasing frustration. They needed to go. Right now. Before the magpies arrived – or worse.

"Can't undo the knots," muttered Orla. "Ah, there we go."

She began unwinding the hessian wrapping and it was too much for Dave. He grabbed the bundle from her hands and scarpered. Orla yelped in surprise, picked up the twine and followed. It was exactly the response he wanted.

Orla noticed the flat tyre when she was still three miles from home. She was on the crest of an escarpment before what she had been hoping would be a long, easy freewheel ride to the coast. Dave leapt from the basket and weed on the grass verge, happy to walk. He'd been dreading that descent.

Orla started pushing, recalling how she'd ignored Uncle Valentine's advice to take a puncture repair kit. Just like she'd ignored his advice about checking the brakes. And not straying into Anna's Wood. Maybe she would listen to him more from now on.

Her spine ached, as though the sacred bundle in her backpack was leaking radiation that was seeping into her bones, so she shrugged the pack off and dropped it into the basket. Instantly the pain shifted from her back to her front. This sprowl was toxic.

Ahead, the weather had turned. Clouds the colour of bruises were bubbling up five miles high over the sea and the wind had switched from a gentle south-westerly to a spiteful, salty blast from the north.

The first raindrops – fat and cold – began falling when Orla and Dave were still a mile from Sicow's Creek, and within a minute the pair were soaked through. Within ten minutes the rain was falling so hard that it hid the marsh, droplets bouncing like ricochets and turning the path to mud and day into night. Rain streaming from his nose, his ears, his tail and his whiskers, Dave had a bad feeling. He kept checking they weren't being followed, especially by those magpies. Maybe they couldn't fly in this weather. But no sooner had he comforted himself with that thought than the trio skittered overhead. With nowhere to perch, they circled, cackling with glee until Orla stamped her foot.

"That's enough," she yelled. "I don't care if you're captains or admirals. I'm not saluting you either. Go home."

The pair tramped across the footbridge to the rope-house, where Orla hid the bundle from St Judith's in a crate of ropes. A witch would find it in seconds, but Orla couldn't bear to have whatever was wrapped in that ancient sackcloth anywhere near her. Not tonight. She locked the door and led Dave back to the house.

Misty and the boys were sitting at the kitchen table. They looked worried.

"UV hasn't come back," Tom told her.

Orla glanced around for somewhere to hang her sodden coat. "Back from where?"

"Out there," he said, pointing towards the distant North Sea.

"It's OK – he knows what he's doing," reasoned Orla. She was looking for the dog towel now.

"Have you seen the weather?" asked Richard.

Orla pointed at her dripping hair and drenched jeans with both hands. "Duh?"

She grabbed the dog towel and made a lunge for Dave. He tried to escape – his preferred method of drying himself was to shake several times, spraying a two-yard radius with mud, and then wipe what was left on carpets and soft furnishings. But Orla was too fast, ignoring his growls and enveloping him in the folds of the smelly old towel.

"He said he'd be back by four," said Misty. She was wearing a long orange cardigan with a shiny red belt that looked, well, odd.

"What time is it now?" asked Orla, releasing Dave, his fur all spiked as though he'd been electrocuted. He ran to the fireplace and began rolling on the rug. Orla picked up his food bowl and began preparing his tea.

Misty frowned. "That's cat food."

"He seems to prefer it these days. Which is good because it's cheaper."

"It's gone seven," said Richard. "I think we should be worried. And there's something else."

"What?" asked Orla, stirring Dave's fish.

"I heard a bell."

Tom nodded. "Me too. It could be the Drowning Bell."

Orla stopped stirring and stared into the sink. She let out a long groan, then reached for her dripping coat. Dave's dinner would have to wait.

"OK," she sighed. "I'll get Mala. You lot grab the rescue gear from the rope-house. It's bound to be a false alarm."

But it wasn't.

CHAPTER 10

Many months previously a backpack mishap had left Malasana soaked in oil of the moon, a multipurpose potion from the book of spells that was especially useful in charms of location – spells conjured to find lost objects. Since then, the rag doll had been responsible for the miraculous rediscovery of dozens of lost treasures – from Richard's iPhone in the woods, at night, to Mum's car keys in a busy multistorey car park and the school cat up a chimney. Mala had never found a person before but it couldn't hurt to try, so here she was, stuffed down the front of Orla's life jacket and leading the search.

The salt marsh was no place for humans or dogs that night. The mud paths were so slippery that the rain alone could push a man off his feet, and the flooded channels looked hungry for human company. The wind whirled like herring gulls, snatching words out of mouths and carrying them far away. The life jackets they'd found with the rescue gear gave them some confidence, and the throwing line

Richard carried meant that if someone did get washed into the creek, they could be rescued. Possibly.

"We should follow this..."

A gust nearly knocked Orla down and she reached for Richard to steady herself, her head torch beam showing only the hectic glitter of rain.

"We need to follow the dyke to the beach," she spluttered.

"Is that you or Mala talking?" asked Richard, wiping the water from his face.

Orla pointed at the rag doll and Richard nodded.

"The waves are in the marsh," shouted Tom.

"The what?" screamed Orla.

"Look," cried Misty, seizing Orla's arm.

Yesterday the dyke had been twelve feet above the creek. Now the channel was inches from the top, threatening to break the bank and wash the search party into the flood.

"This is madness!" bellowed Richard.

"Uncle Valentine!" yelled Orla into the thieving wind. "Uncle Valentine!"

Dave agreed with Richard. The waves washing over the kids' boots were big enough to sweep him away and he was digging his claws into the mud to stay upright. The wind and the rain had washed away any chance of tracking the old man by smell. He glanced at what had been a soggy tidal swamp and was now a storm-tossed lake, really hoping he wouldn't have to swim tonight.

"Look out!" cried Tom.

A black shape was racing down the creek, betrayed only by the faint trail of white as its crest broke across the dyke. Orla lunged for the big handle on Dave's harness as the wave hit, and missed. It was only knee-deep on humans, but enough to carry Dave away. He swam with it, using his tail as a rudder to steer himself back to the bank and sneezing with irritation as he dragged himself onto land.

"That could have been us," said Richard as Dave rejoined them, shaking in a vain attempt to get dry.

Orla bent down to lift him but Dave pushed past. He needed to get this rescue mission over with before the rescuers needed rescuing. As he pressed ahead, nose down in vain hope of a scent, Orla felt Mala being pulled, as though by a magnet. Then she saw the light: a faint yellow glow like a candle in the storm.

It was two hundred yards ahead on the far side of the flooded creek: a head torch bobbing as its owner struggled to lift a body into a skiff.

"You stupid, stupid children!" screamed the owner: a tall woman in shiny black waterproofs. "Turn back now!"

"Is that Uncle Valentine?" called Orla.

"Wave coming," warned Tom, grabbing Orla's belt with one hand and Dave's harness with the other.

"Turn back, you idiots. You'll all drown." A flash lit up her face, the thunder like a bomb blast.

The wave hit, deeper and more powerful than the first.

"Who is that woman?" asked Misty.

"It's the postmistress," replied Orla. She cupped her hands around her mouth. "Is that Uncle Valentine?" she cried again.

"Of course it is," snapped the postmistress. "I can't get him into the boat."

"We can help," shouted Orla. "Row over to us."

"And let your uncle go? Get out of here before the sea kills you all."

Orla looked at the channel, then at Richard. "I could swim it," she said.

"Don't be an idiot," he warned, wincing as a gust of rain hit him like a handful of grit. "You'll drown."

"You will actually drown," agreed Misty. "Use the line."

"Stand back," ordered Richard, taking position on the dyke, his legs astride. Holding the coil of rope in his left hand, he whirled the weighted end around his head like a cowboy determined to lasso a steer. Then he let fly. The rope flew straight up in the air and came down on his head.

"Out of the way," sighed Misty, snatching the line.

Her first throw had the range, but was blown off course

by the wind. So was the second, and the third, and by now the postmistress was shouting that she couldn't hold on to Uncle Valentine any longer.

"Let me have another go," insisted Richard.

"Stay out of it," ordered Misty, hurling the rope a fourth time.

As it fell wide, no one heard the faint splash of a Jack Russell throwing himself into the water. He swam until he hit the rope, gripped it between his teeth and set a course for the skiff.

"Dog off the starboard bow," shouted Misty.

The postmistress looked over her shoulder and, gripping Uncle Valentine's life jacket with her right hand, held her left overboard. As Dave came close, waves breaking over his face, she snatched the line.

"Drag him aboard," called Orla.

"Absolutely not," cried the witch.

Unbelievable, thought Dave. He took a deep breath, performed a U-turn and paddled for shore.

Back at Sicow's Creek they laid the old man on the Afghan rug. Seawater ran from his nose, ears and fingers, pooling on the carpet. Misty kneeled on one side, feeling for a pulse. Orla kneeled on the other, feeling utterly useless, while Richard and Tom wandered the house in vain search of a phone signal. Elizabeth Edwards emptied the contents of her bag on the kitchen table and threw Orla a vicious look.

"This is your fault," she hissed. "As soon as I heard the Drowning Bell, I knew this was your work." She slammed a leather pouch onto the table. "And now the dying has started, thanks to your meddling."

Orla felt a hot rush of anger. Or was it shame?

"There's no pulse," announced Misty. "Can you bring him back?"

Orla rummaged one-handed in her backpack for her book of spells. She couldn't help shaking slightly. "I need to look it up," she said. "I don't know the ritual."

"I thought it just came to you when you needed it, like magic."

"It used to," she admitted. "But not here. I think it's the salt water." She gripped Uncle Valentine's cold, wet hand between hers. "We should try CPR," she said.

"It's too late for that," barked the postmistress. "He's been in the water for at least an hour."

"Will one of you do something?" shouted Misty. "You're both witches, for goodness' sake. Reviving those taken by the sea is supposed to be an entry level skill."

"If I could, I would," retorted the postmistress. "But I need sprowl."

"Are you serious?" asked Misty.

"I came out in such a hurry…"

Tom appeared, staring fearfully at the body. "Is he actually dead?"

"Maybe we can improvise," said the postmistress, glancing anxiously around the kitchen. She lifted the crystal from around her neck and stared at it. "There's some sprowl in this," she said. "But not enough."

She picked up the yellow teacup from the table. "What are these?"

"They're the stones the magpie brought me," said Orla.

The postmistress sniffed them. "Bingo."

"No, they don't have any sprowl," argued Orla. "I'd have noticed."

"But you didn't," retorted the postmistress. "Anyway, there's not enough. Did you find any at the churches?"

Orla gasped and nodded. "It's in the rope-house."

"Well, fetch it then, you stupid girl."

"Witches," muttered Misty in frustration.

As Orla ran for the door, Richard came clattering down the stairs. "I need to go to the—"

He didn't finish. Dave was lying across the third step from the bottom and, as Richard descended, he stood up and Richard tripped over him, colliding with the display cabinet. The emperor's clock slid off it like a dislodged boulder, landed on Uncle Valentine's chest with a sickening

123

thud, bounced and then shattered into a hundred pieces as it hit the floor. A final, feeble tinkle filled the horrified silence.

"Oh no!" gasped Richard.

"I'm surrounded by clowns!" wailed Misty as green water sprayed from the corpse's mouth.

The postmistress pointed at Orla, her bun unpinned and her hair falling like eels around her face. "All this chaos is down to you, girl," she hissed. "Mark my words. And this dear man's death is only the first you've caused."

An eruption of coughing filled the room.

"I'm not bloody dead," spluttered Uncle Valentine. "Where's my rum?"

CHAPTER 11

The one-footed magpie fluttered onto the windowsill and tapped on the glass at 5.32 a.m. For a moment, Orla kept her eyes squeezed shut, hoping last night was all a crazy dream. Then she sighed, swung her legs out of bed and opened the window. The storm had passed, but the cool salty air that rushed in still smelled of chaos.

"Good morning, Captain," she muttered. "Why do you keep coming here? I don't trust you one bit."

The bird tipped her head to one side then the other, completely unruffled, then dropped a white stone on the windowsill and hopped into the sky. Orla left the window open and shuffled to Uncle Valentine's room. Dave was sitting beside the door, his tail wagging. The postmistress had stayed over to take turns with Orla keeping watch on the patient and had been unable to stop the Jack Russell standing guard. She hadn't said a word until she put on her coat to leave at 4.30 a.m., speaking only to leave strict instructions for his care.

First, the patient was confined to bed. Second, he was to drink six cups of a special herbal tea every day. This, said the postmistress with a knowing glance, would make it easier to keep him in bed. Third, if he took a turn for the worse, Orla was to call the number written on the pad beside the bed. Fourth, if he showed any signs of improvement, then Orla, her brothers, Misty and Uncle Valentine were never to call the postmistress or visit her ever again.

On this last matter, she had been very clear, Orla recalled. Scratching her head, she checked on her brothers. Tom wasn't there. Richard had grown long black hair and was wearing camouflage pyjamas.

"He gave up his bed for me," said Misty. "He's on the sofa downstairs."

"Very chivalrous," muttered Orla. "Did you sleep well?"

"Sleep?" Misty laughed. "I've been working all night. Heard you stomping around too. How's the patient?"

"Unconscious and snoring." She noticed the reporter's notebook on the bed, the screwed-up balls of paper all over the floor. "I can't get used to you not being Raven," she admitted.

Misty sat up, her back against the headboard. "I'm still me."

"Why can't you just be yourself?"

"Because Joan Baqri gets nothing done. She's a loser and a victim."

"Do you seriously think that?" asked Orla. It was as rare to hear her friend use her real name as it was sad to hear how she saw herself.

"You should look after yourself rather than worrying about me," snapped Misty. "Have you ever wondered how this weird life is affecting you?"

Orla shrugged. "Not really. I just get on with stuff."

Misty shook her head. "Last night that stuff included surviving a near-hurricane and bringing your uncle back from the dead. And there'll be worse to come, Orla Perry."

"There will," Orla replied more seriously. "But what can I do?"

"You need to start looking after yourself. And remember: you're not bulletproof."

"I know."

"I don't think you do," sighed Misty. "But whatever. We need to talk about the big news that Richard and I found out yesterday."

"After I've made Uncle Valentine his tea," said Orla. She paused by the bedroom door. "Oh, and if you were a loser and a victim, I would never have asked you to help me. So there, Joan."

Downstairs all was tidy. The postmistress had seen to

that, and the only mess was the remains of Tom's breakfast: a can of Tizer and two Mars bars.

"Where is he?" asked Orla.

"Went out," mumbled Richard from beneath the blanket on the sofa. "Wanted to see the beach. He couldn't persuade Dave to go, though."

Orla nodded, dropping the new stone into the yellow teacup. "Dave's on guard duty." She filled the kettle, put it on the stove and tipped a teaspoon of herbs into a tin mug. She looked out of the window, across the marsh to where Tom was running along the sea dyke. From here he looked excited rather than scared, but you couldn't be sure of anything around here.

She opened the door, whistled once and Dave came thumping down the stairs. "Go get Tom, dog," she said. "Escort him home."

Misty followed Dave down. "How are you feeling, Richard?" she called.

"Oh, you know," said Richard. "The usual Perry family holiday feeling, of extreme trauma and impending doom. Last night was a nightmare."

The kettle whistled. Orla poured water onto the herbs, added a teaspoon of honey and stirred. She left the mug beside Uncle Valentine's bed and came back downstairs.

"We've got good news for you, witch girl," announced Richard.

"Can't wait," said Orla.

"There's no gas," Misty told her.

"Not in Anna's Wood, at least," added Richard. "The gas-bearing rocks are under this marsh."

Orla stared at them. Tom's footsteps were thumping up the wooden steps. "You what?" she said.

Tom and Dave burst through the doorway.

"We found a survey from six years ago," said Misty.

"UV's boat is on the beach," cried Tom.

"There's nothing but chalk and flint beneath that wood," said Richard.

"It's smashed to bits," continued Tom. "Shall I go and tell him?"

Orla put a hand on his arm. "Best not," she said softly. She gave Richard and Misty a fierce, disbelieving look. "How can there be no gas?" She spun round, nearly stepping on Dave, and pointed west. "Why is that yellow army going to destroy the wood and kill all those beautiful birds if there's no gas?"

Richard shrugged. "Dunno."

"It doesn't matter why," added Misty. "All we know is that GasFrac's lied and if we can prove it, we can shut them down. How much sprowl did you find, just in case?"

Orla swallowed. "Some." She ran a nervous glance around the kitchen. "Not sure how much."

Could he who heard everything be listening in right now?

"Did the magpie bring a stone?" asked Tom.

Orla nodded. "A white one today."

"I've got a theory," began Tom, but Orla stopped him.

"Save it for later," she said, grabbing her backpack. "Let's go outside."

A few moments later, the five stood on the bridge over the creek in the watery sunshine. A chilly breeze ruffled the marsh.

"Um, why are we here?" asked Richard. "We've left a perfectly warm house to stand in a freezing swamp."

"Because it's safer," said Orla. She nodded down at the tidal creek ebbing beneath the bridge. "Look – salt water, oak timbers and a crossing over water. A triple barrier to his magic."

"Whose magic?" asked Misty. She was the only one who didn't feel the cold.

Orla shrugged. "I don't know. The postmistress is scared to death of someone who hears everything but she refused to give me a name. I'm pretty sure that he's connected to GasFrac, though."

"So, if there's no gas down there, what are they mining?" asked Richard, rubbing his arms.

"Maybe treasure?" suggested Tom, but no one was listening to him.

"And there's another thing," said Orla. "Someone has been carving letters into the churches around here. DAL. It's done really neatly, like the inscriptions on gravestones."

"I think we've got more serious crimes to investigate than neatly done vandalism," sniffed Misty. She looked hard at Orla. "You're sweating. Are you all right?"

"I'm OK," replied Orla. "But I think I'm allergic to sprowl now. I can feel it, but it hurts." She looked at Tom. "There's a heavy thing wrapped in sackcloth hidden in that big crate in the rope-house. It's stored sprowl from St Judith's Church. Can you take it to the smokehouse and hide it somewhere safe?"

"We're not allowed in the smokehouse," Richard pointed out.

Orla shrugged. "I don't care," she said firmly. "I need this somewhere safe and dry that's near enough if I need it and far enough that I can't feel it. Off you go, Tom."

"Then can we go to the beach so I can show you the wreck?" he asked.

"Go to the beach?" cried Misty. "There's too much work to do. We need to find out why GasFrac lied, and get the message out that whatever's happening at Anna's Wood, it's not about the gas."

"There's a library with Internet access in King's Lynn," said Richard. "I could catch the Coasthopper and do some research there."

Orla gave Misty a hard stare. "What did you just say?"

"We need to get the message out."

"After that."

"It's not about the gas."

"Yes!" cried Orla. "It was in my dream. I made notes." She rummaged in her backpack for her notebook.

"Speaking of dreams," said Richard. "I dreamed of an amazing shopping centre last night. You could get anything you wanted for free."

"Thanks for that," sighed Orla. "Can we—"

"Hang on a minute," said Tom. "I dreamed of a shopping centre too. Did yours have a rollercoaster?"

"No," said Richard, "but do you remember what Uncle Valentine said the other night?"

Orla froze. "'All we dream of around here is a shopping centre … and a country park,'" she said slowly.

"Exactly," said Richard.

"Country park?" asked Misty. "Last night I dreamed I was on a rowing boat on a lake in a beautiful country park."

Orla continued rummaging in her backpack. Where was that notebook? She pulled out old tissues, a folded page from a newspaper and an ancient letter from school about a long-passed event that she'd forgotten to give to Mum.

"Jemima Water-Mills said that everyone has the same dreams these days." Next came a walnut, the coil of blackthorn twigs, a red bandana, some copper wire, her penknife, surgical gloves and a small willow wand. "I thought she meant everyone dreams of being an influencer like her, or a billionaire, but..." She looked at the others in despair. "I've lost my notebook."

She replayed yesterday in her mind: the post office. The church down the muddy track. The ruin by the roadside. The magnificent temple to nature in which she'd found the bundle. "I left it at St Judith's. I need to go back."

"And we need to go to King's Lynn," said Richard.

Tom folded his arms. "I'm staying here."

"Me too," said Misty. "Can you fetch dinner, Richard?"

"Burgers, please," added Tom. "Or pizza."

It took Orla fifteen minutes to repair yesterday's puncture and fifty-five minutes to pedal over the hill to Wissenby. There was no birdsong today, and no traffic but for a single black SUV that forced Orla and Dave onto the grass verge. Three magpies swept in from the left as they descended into the silent village, and at St Judith's they found only mystery, disappointment and anxiety.

The slab beneath which Orla had found the bundle had a new marking.

DAL

And the notebook was gone.

CHAPTER 12

Back at Sicow's Creek, Tom had shown Misty an old printing machine he'd found in the workshop and the pair had spent the morning getting it working. Throbbing with disappointment and anger at her carelessness, Orla was only half listening to her friend's excited chatter.

"It's called a mimeograph," said Misty. "You make a stencil, stick it on this drum, turn the handle and..."

Orla watched as a sheet of paper was sucked through the machine, appearing on the other side as a poster saying:

PEOPLE OF NORFOLK
YOU HAVE BEEN MISLED
THERE IS NO GAS AT ANNA'S WOOD

"Very cool," said Orla. "But can we prove it?"

"We don't need to," said Misty. "It's all there in black and white in the survey."

"Do you have the survey?" asked Orla.

Misty smiled. "No, but I can tell you where to find it."

"If I could find it, could GasFrac find it too?"

Misty's smile vanished. "Oh my God," she gasped. "I need to go back to Cromer." She dashed out of the workshop, then ran back in to grab a pile of posters, a hammer and a jar of shiny nails.

"Back later," she called.

Orla studied the shelves for a moment. One of her dad's favourite sayings was "You have to know before you can see", and it was so true. To anyone who didn't know, Uncle Valentine's habit of keeping nails in old jam jars was just practical recycling. To one who did know, it was evidence of the craft, because these were witching jars offering basic defence against evil intent. She picked seven jars, packed them into her backpack and went outside into the sunshine. She could see Misty in the distance, running through the marsh towards the bus stop.

"Where's she off to?"

Orla turned to see Tom at her side.

"Back to Cromer. She forgot something."

"Wow," he said. "I didn't think she ever forgot anything. Anyway, congratulations – it's a mermaid."

"What's a mermaid?" asked Orla. She felt cold and shivery and her fingers were numb.

"That thing you found. It's a mermaid carved from

136

ivory. Maybe walrus tusk. It was in a wooden box and sort of padded out with these red felt things."

"These red felt things are charm purses," said Orla. "They keep her safe."

"Whatever." He shrugged. "There's a massive chest of drawers in the smokehouse. I've hidden her in there and tied the red string around the knob so you know which one, because there's like a hundred different drawers. You should check them out. They're full of those herbs and stones and stuff you lot use. And there's something else. It's about those little stones your magpie brings you."

"Later, Tom," said Orla distractedly. "I've got to check on Uncle Valentine."

Tom sighed. "Do you need Dave?" he asked.

"Why?"

"Can I take him to the beach?"

Suddenly Orla felt guilty. All Tom wanted was an ordinary holiday doing simple things like playing with his dog at the seaside. "Of course you can." She smiled. "Just don't drown or Mum will kill me."

Uncle Valentine wasn't a pretty sight – two black eyes, a split lip and a broken nose – but at least he was conscious, lying propped up on his pillow and listening to the radio. The 1 p.m. bulletin was reporting that tech companies were blaming a cyber-attack for the collapse of Internet service in a wide area of the east of England, and Uncle Valentine was chuckling.

"Let's see how they all manage without their Wi-Fi," he rasped.

"Glad to see you're well enough to laugh at the misfortune of others," said Orla.

"Their own fault," retorted Uncle Valentine. "Humanity created something it can't live without, and if it wasn't so scary it would be even funnier." He struggled to sit up. "I need to get out of here," he growled. "There's work to do."

"Nothing that can't wait," said Orla. She put a mug of herbal tea on the bedside cabinet and leaned in close to get a better look at his pupils. "You've had a bash on the head and got possible broken ribs, so you need to stay put for a few days." She quietly placed one jar of nails on his bedside table, another on the chest of drawers, and a third on the floor beside the door. In his concussed state he probably wouldn't notice.

"Don't be filling my house with your witch bottles," muttered Uncle Valentine. "I had enough of that with Liz the Whizz." He started to swing his legs out of bed, then stopped with a long groan.

"That reminds me," said Orla. "You've hurt your back too."

"Flipping boat came down on top of me," he gasped.

"The postmistress ordered bed rest."

"She used to be a nurse, you know," said Uncle Valentine.

Orla sat on the edge of the bed. "Did she live here?"

"For a while, yes," admitted Uncle Valentine. "Then she left."

"Why?"

"Wasn't my fault," he wheezed. "I'm the easiest man on earth to live with. She went because of what she is. A witch's destiny is to be alone with her secrets." He rolled a pair of bloodshot eyes towards Orla. "Mark my words, girl. That's an extraordinary gift you've got, but it comes at a high cost."

Orla picked at her jeans. "I know it's an extraordinary gift," she said. "But it's hard work. Sometimes I wish I was normal."

Uncle Valentine's chuckle became a hacking cough. "No, you don't. You're a fighter. A solver of mysteries and a warrior for justice. If you didn't have your witchcraft to rely on, you'd still be the same. You know I'm right."

"S'pose," she mumbled. She looked up. "Tom says the smokehouse is full of witchcraft stuff. Does it belong to Elizabeth Edwards?"

Uncle Valentine sighed. "It does. I should have locked it all away. It's too late now, and I doubt she'll be back for it."

Orla stood up to leave. "Drink your tea. It's made with herbs to help you sleep."

"First off, that's not tea. It's water with weeds in," muttered Uncle Valentine. "Second off, bring me my rum."

Orla put her hands on her hips. "Drink the tea first. Then we'll see about the rum."

The smokehouse was a windowless building of flint and ancient brick supported on the trunks of black oaks thrust deep into the marsh. Orla pushed open the heavy door, instantly smelling the odours of the craft. Blinking in the darkness, she sat Malasana – still wet from the storm – on the workbench and lit candles so she could see, noticing the pot-bellied stove and flue, the high shelves lined with pots and jars and the beams hung with bones. There were gwelens of yew and hornbeam and willow, and bundles of dried botanicals, an old oak table and a huge apothecary's cabinet – its drawers full of what Tom had so accurately described as "herbs and stones and stuff".

But how, wondered Orla, could the postmistress have conjured charms in a room stood on a tidal marsh? There had to be a shield or insulation of some sort. There was a copper strip along the door lintel, its green crust proof of the salt it had soaked up, but would that be enough? She dropped to her knees to examine the floor. Beneath a mantle of dust, it was smooth, warm to the touch and smelled like medicine.

"Palo santo," she whispered. "That's the Spanish for holy wood, Mala. It's the densest wood in the world."

Malasana didn't need the translation. She came from Madrid.

But this was more than a floor. The wood was inlaid with the perfect circle of the witch's compass and marked with the magical gates of east, south, west and north. At each gate was carved an image of its guardian spirit: the serpent, the hare, the toad and the crow. The stove stood dead centre in the circle, and around the outside were carved the words of the rite of purification, which had to be performed before any conjuration to make sure no evil polluted the magic.

Orla climbed slowly to her feet, gaping in astonishment. This wasn't a shed of spells; it was a laboratory of advanced magic, hidden in a place no witch hunter would ever think to look. There were history and mystery in this building, but any investigation would have to wait because, right now, Orla needed to protect Sicow's Creek against he who heard everything.

She lit the stove and leafed through her Cornish book of spells. To return a curse; a rite of hallows; the clootie charm; conjuration of the witch fire; the Traumnebel; a hex against spies...

That was the one. And a blasting against evil ... the workings of protection – there were lots of good spells here.

Orla began rummaging through the drawers of the apothecary's cabinet. Malasana sat beside her, softening the toxic effect of the sprowl radiating from the mermaid. But not enough.

First, she performed the rite of purification, reading the sacred words as she paced the circle in the sinistral – or anticlockwise – direction. Then, swallowing back the feeling that she was going to be sick and ignoring her aching bones, Orla bit her lip and went to work. She untied the red string from the mermaid's drawer and turned to a page in her book of spells entitled "A Working Against Prying". An hour later, the thread was knotted, hung with one hundred and five dried rowan berries, wrapped around a twig of dried briar and dusted with witch powder. Balancing on a chair, she looped it over a hook in the beam above the pot-bellied stove.

Next, she took the coiled blackthorn twigs from her backpack, tied them into spiky circles and hung them from the same hook. Then, blinking from her headache, she opened and shut what felt like a thousand tiny drawers, tipping pine needles, orange buckthorn berries and lead-like sloes into a small cauldron. She shaved wormwood into the mix with her penknife and added patchouli, rue, colophony, dragon's blood and grated madder root. The potion was reacting to the presence of sprowl even before Orla began the incantation: fizzing and popping as its magic was released.

Leaving the mixture to prove, Orla made an ounce of banishing ink, another of crow's watch powder – swapping the henbane for horehound – and half a cup of fire of Mars. In the back of the book of spells there were several pages blank but for the handwritten advice *this paper is for use in charms*. Ripping out all but one, she tore each of the magic sheets into four squares, picked a crow's feather from a drawer full of quills, dipped it in the banishing ink and wrote the same message on each:

What words are spoken within these walls are blessed and protected by these signs and whosoever seeks to overhear shall be thwarted by this charm.

On the back of each square she wrote:

```
S   A   T   O   R
A   R   E   P   O
T   E   N   E   T
O   P   E   R   A
R   O   T   A   S
```

This was another powerful charm, magical whatever way you read it. Carefully she placed each slip of paper into an envelope of red felt with a pinch of crow's watch powder, stitched it closed with black thread, placed each in a net sack and then hung them all alongside the rowan berry cord and the blackthorn. Then she carried the cauldron to the stove, took blackthorn chips from one drawer and a silver teaspoon from another. Finally she took a deep breath, gritted her teeth, removed the carved mermaid from her hiding place and laid her down at the east gate of the compass, where serpent spirit could drink her magic.

The pain was almost unbearable, shooting up her arms like axe blows, and it took several minutes to subside. Breathing hard, her brow glistening with sweat in the candlelight, Orla glanced at the rag doll.

"We're ready, Mala. Hold your breath."

She pulled her red bandana from her backpack, tied it around her face and dropped the blackthorn chips onto the hotplate. As they began to smoulder, she dripped the potion from the silver spoon onto the glowing embers, creating a dense cloud of purple smoke that rose, wreathed the charms and impregnated them with protective magic. Her eyes streaming, Orla stretched her arms out wide like a proper witch and called:

"Serpent smoke, empower my workings. Protect and strengthen these charms to guard against the ears of eavesdroppers, the hands of evil and the eyes of spies. Know that this must be the will of Bucca Dhu, and keep us safe as long as you linger."

Back in the house, all was quiet, but for how long Orla didn't know, so she worked fast because the rules said such charms had to be unseen and yet seen. That meant no one could see you putting them in position, but they had to be able to notice them afterwards. The charms hung, and he who heard everything banished, Orla flopped exhausted onto her bed with damp Mala at her side, and closed her eyes. Just for a second...

CHAPTER 13

Orla woke as night was falling: suddenly, painfully, and glancing around in horror before jumping to her feet, checking on Uncle Valentine – who was in as deep a sleep as she had just been – and running down the stairs.

Richard looked up from his television repair job and raised an eyebrow. "Oh look," he said. "Sleeping Beauty has awoken."

"I just lay down for a second," said Orla. "I can't believe I fell asleep."

"You must have needed it," observed Misty. She lifted a Manila folder from the table and let it drop. "Look what I got while you were sleeping. Want to go outside and discuss it?"

Orla nodded at the red felt envelopes taped above each window, the blackthorn charms and the red rope of rowan berries hanging above the door. "We can talk in here," she said. "They're charms against eavesdropping and evil intent."

Only Tom, it seemed, had seen the charms. "I thought it was Christmas," he commented.

Orla rubbed her eyes and looked at the folder. "You copied the entire file?"

"No. This is the entire file," said Misty with a grin. "It seemed prudent to take all the evidence into protective custody."

"She means she stole it," explained Tom.

"Brilliant," said Orla. She filled a glass with tap water and downed it in three huge gulps. "How was the beach?"

"It was OK," said Tom. "Can I tell you about the stones now?"

"Let's hear from Richard first."

Richard glanced fearfully around the kitchen. "You sure it's safe to talk?"

Orla nodded. "I think so. They're pretty powerful workings."

"Fine," said Richard. "The Internet went down at lunchtime. Some kind of cyber-attack the librarian said, but I made some pretty weird discoveries before then." He swiped his phone and began reading from his notes. "First off, Anna's Wood is GasFrac's only UK site. But they're also building extraction plants in Venezuela, Namibia, Spain, Mexico and France..."

"Can we focus on Anna's Wood for now?" asked Orla.

147

"Perhaps you should be more global in your thinking," retorted Richard. He had that smug look on his face that meant he was about to say something very clever. "I googled the exact locations of the thirteen sites where GasFrac is operating worldwide and used them as a search string. Guess what came up?"

"An article in *Fracking Weekly*?" hazarded Misty.

"More than that. Loads of scary reports of protests, arrests and disappearances – and something else." He paused for dramatic effect.

"Get on with it, Miss Marple," urged Orla.

"You've heard of the Treskaidekastron? It's the ancient Greek name for a thirteen-pointed star."

"Nope," said Orla.

"Oh my God," gasped Misty. "Is Anna's Wood one of the points?"

"See, witch girl?" Richard smirked. "This is what people who don't spend afternoons in bed are like. And yes, Misty, you're right. Sort of. Back in the sixties psychic researchers did the maths and guessed there must be a point around here. Since then, satellite imagery has made it millions of times easier to pinpoint exact positions, and because the entire world thinks it's all crackpot pseudoscience, no one has noticed what GasFrac is really up to."

Tom had been ransacking a cupboard for biscuits.

"What exactly is he talking about, Orla?" he asked.

"I have no idea," she replied. A sudden gust rattled the windows. Was *he* listening, or were the charms working?

Richard waved at Misty. "You tell them. Best to do it in simple words, as though you're talking to five-year-olds."

Misty brought Uncle Valentine's ink-spotted globe to the table, set it down and spun it. "This is the world. As it spins, it generates an energy that witches call sprowl. Scientists call it the telluric current." She looked at Orla and Tom to check they were following. "The principle is very simple: think of the planet as a bike with a dynamo that creates electricity as it moves." She traced her fingers over the surface in a series of crazy swirls. "Some people think this energy flows in circles. Others believe it flows in straight lines."

"Ley lines," added Richard.

"Exactly," said Misty. "Most magicians think of sprowl as a river in constant flow. The Zoroastrians thought differently. They saw sprowl as pulses of intense energy, zooming around like subterranean comets. If you could capture the comets, you'd have unimaginable magic power – but you can't, because first, they're moving at the speed of light; and second, you never know where they're going to be."

"How do you know all this?" asked Tom.

"Because I study the shady stuff that others don't see,"

replied Misty. She touched a finger on the globe and brought it to a stop. "The Zoroastrians also believed that sprowl didn't follow random paths. Their theory was it travelled between thirteen fixed points on the world's surface that formed a perfect star."

She opened her notebook, drew thirteen points in a circle and joined them to make a star. "There are something like three hundred trillion possible routes the sprowl can take within this star, so being in the right place at the right time is almost impossible. But if you find a point, all you have to do is wait. And if you find all thirteen points, you've got direct access to unlimited magical power 24/7/365." She slapped the globe, sending it into a whirl. "Own the Treskaidekastron and you own the world."

"But there's no sprowl at Anna's Wood," argued Orla.

"There must be," retorted Misty. "Why else would they be here?"

Orla sat back in her chair, her mind spinning like the globe. "Who the heck are we up against?"

Misty put the globe back on the chest of drawers. "That's what we need to find out," she said. "Does anyone want a drink?"

"I'll have a Coke," called Richard. "There's a big bottle outside on the step."

"Me too," added Tom.

Orla looked at Richard. "Amazing work," she said. "Thank you."

He shrugged. "It was pretty easy. I would have found out loads more if the Web hadn't gone down, but I did work out what DAL stands for while I was on the bus to King's Lynn. I googled 'DAL, churches and carvings' and it led to an article in yesterday's *Eastern Daily Press* about a spate of vandalism in Norfolk churches. They thought it was a new thing, but then I found a piece from National Geographic in 1973." He swiped his phone and spun it round so Orla could see. "This picture was taken in the Church of the Nativity in Bethlehem. See the carving on the wall?"

"DAL!" cried Orla. "That's exactly it!"

"Aha," said Richard. He was going to be smug again. "It stands for Dominium Antiquae Legionis. Property of the Old Legion."

Two full glasses of Coke hit the floor and exploded. Misty turned from the kitchen counter. She didn't even realize she had dropped them.

"Uh-oh," she whispered. "We're in trouble."

"What did we do?" asked Tom, looking guilty.

There was another crash as something heavy hit the door. The house shook with the impact and Dave went ballistic. Proper hedgehog-haired, wolverine-toothed, honey-badger fury, throwing himself at the door as though he could punch through it with his nose. Richard grabbed a poker from the fireplace, and Tom a wooden spoon, because that was all he could find at short notice. Misty folded her arms and Orla sidled around the table to kill the lights and peek out of the kitchen window.

"There's no one there," she said. "Tom, grab Dave and hold him tight."

"Don't go out there," cried Richard. He leaned close to Misty. "Is it the Old Legion?"

Misty glanced at the poker in his trembling hand. "If it is, that's going to be as much use as a courgette in a gunfight."

"Who exactly are they?"

"I'll tell you later," said Misty.

As Orla opened the door, Tom struggled to hold on to Dave and failed. The Jack Russell shot out onto the porch like a rocket-propelled grenade, screeching to a halt on the third step down as he noticed, as Orla had done, that there was no one there. Just a burning smell and a large stone. He sniffed it and recoiled – it was as hot as a rock thrown straight from hell – then looked around suspiciously. The thrower might be hidden beneath the house, so Dave put his nose to the ground and went into stealth mode.

"Careful, dog," whispered Orla. The white light from the GasFrac compound was ruining her night vision. Anyone could be out there. She shrugged helplessly and bent to touch the stone. She too was burned, but she saw what Dave couldn't. The image packed inside ripped across her retinas like the afterglow of fireworks: an elegant Victorian hotel on the edge of the salt marsh with a sign in blood-red neon flashing on its roof:

You and Me:
Tea at Three
xXx

Orla had the sudden sensation of moving backwards at high speed, of the entire world falling away and leaving her the only speck of consciousness in the entire universe. She gripped the handrail to steady herself and stared at the moon until the vertigo subsided.

"Dave," she called softly. "Call off the search."

Whoever had thrown that stone didn't need to hide under houses to scare people.

CHAPTER 14

"Ah," said Uncle Valentine. "I recognize it now. That's the Stannard Hotel in St Stannard." He looked at Orla's sketch again. "That's a pretty good picture."

He'd probably recognized it the first time she'd shown him, thought Orla, but he'd insisted that another tot of rum would jog his memory.

"The whole place has been completely taken over by GasFrac," continued Uncle Valentine. "It's become Mr Thorn's personal residence."

"Have you met him?" asked Orla.

Uncle Valentine shook his head. "He's too important to mix with the common people. I've seen him about, though: he's a short fellow with shiny black hair and painted nails. They say he's got eyes as black as the grave, but I've never been close enough to notice. He's driven around in a black SUV – silent as a phantom." He threw a glance at Misty. "I'll have another tot of rum now, please, Miss Meadows – and pour one for yourself. You look like you need it."

"Not yet," breathed Misty. She left the room then returned with her satchel. She shuffled through a stack of photos, pulled out two and laid them on the bed. The first showed a short man with shiny hair and painted nails in a black suit shaking hands with the French president. The second showed the same man on the phone on the steps of the United Nations building in New York.

Uncle Valentine nodded. "That's him."

Misty clasped the pictures to her chest and flopped onto the bed. She looked at the floor, then at Orla, then at Uncle Valentine. She looked out of the window into the glare from the compound, then looked at the floor again.

"He's operating in plain sight because no one ever learns," she mumbled. Her eyes flickered back and forth as if watching the events of the near future.

"You know what I think we should do?" she said at last. "I think we should grab our stuff and run away right now, because that's the only way I can see us getting out of this place alive."

"Who exactly is Mr Thorn?" asked Orla, glancing around the room. At least she had a name now for he who heard everything.

"He's Balin Angramainyu – a Grand Magus and one of the Seven Knights of the Old Legion," said Misty. "He's calling himself Godric Thorn now, like he called himself

Cyprian, Baal Shem and the Count of St Germain at various times in history."

"He always seemed a bit shifty to me," agreed Uncle Valentine.

"How do you know it's him?" asked Orla.

"Because there are always people looking for him. Looking for all of them. But they always disappear." Misty crossed to the bedroom door. "Richard, Tom? Come up here, please, and bring that bottle of rum."

"What's going on?" asked Tom as he entered. "This has gone from tedious to freaking terrifying in, like, one hour."

"We've made the connection," said Misty. "And it's not good. The guy who runs GasFrac is a Knight of the Old Legion."

"What exactly *is* this Old Legion?" asked Richard.

"I think they're wizards of some sort," said Orla.

"That's like saying the Death Star is a spaceship of some sort," sniffed Misty. "The Old Legion is an ancient order of magicians dating back to the fourth century. The organized religions had tried to eradicate witchcraft, but the most powerful magi survived, living alongside the kings and queens, the popes and the chieftains. They can start wars, cause famines and conjure pandemics."

"So they're quite scary?" asked Tom.

"The Seven Knights of the Old Legion are the scariest people on earth," said Misty solemnly. "And Godric Thorn, as he calls himself now, is one of them."

"What's he got to do with GasFrac?" wondered Tom.

Everyone, including Dave, looked at him, waiting for the Treskaidekastron penny to drop. It took a moment but then his eyes widened and his jaw dropped. "Oh my God," he exclaimed. "He wants to control all the sprowl!"

"Exactly," said Misty. "The Seven Knights of the Old Legion detest one another. They have done for centuries, but their fear and hatred have stopped any one of them becoming more powerful than the others – and that has kept the world safe. Well, sort of. You can't imagine what it would be like if just one of them was in charge."

"Are they all like Godric Thorn?" asked Tom.

"Not really," said Misty. "Four of them are women. But they're all immeasurably powerful."

"And immortal?" asked Uncle Valentine.

Misty shrugged. "We don't know how that works." She pulled another picture from her bag. "This is a painting of the Count of St Germain in 1748, without the powdered wig. Look like anybody we know?"

Uncle Valentine nodded. "That's him all right."

"Presumably the Old Legion is immeasurably evil too?" murmured Richard. He looked depressed.

Misty frowned. "They're sort of beyond good and evil. They're so focused on destroying one another that they don't really notice what happens to those who get caught in the crossfire."

"But if Godric Thorn has found all thirteen points, does that mean he can control all the sprowl in the world?" asked Tom.

"Yep," said Orla.

"And what happens to the other six?"

"They disappear or they die," said Misty. "And then Godric can basically shorten his name to God."

"OK." Tom nodded. "Er, can I ask one more question?"

"No," said Misty.

"Hear him out," insisted Uncle Valentine. "He's asking all the right ones so far."

"What exactly are we going to do about it? We're just a bunch of kids and a half-drowned old man – no offence, Uncle Valentine. Isn't this actually a job for the army?"

"He's got a point," said Uncle Valentine. "Pass me that bottle, someone."

"No," said Orla firmly.

"If Godric takes the Treskaidekastron, no army will be able to defeat him," said Misty.

"So we need to stop him," stated Orla.

"I presume you have a cunning plan?" asked Richard, handing the bottle to Uncle Valentine.

"Not really," said Orla, snatching the rum from Uncle Valentine. "He's invited me to tea tomorrow so I'm going to ask him politely to reconsider."

"You're crazy!" spluttered Richard. "He'll kill you."

"I don't think so. If he wanted to kill me, he'd have done so already."

"She's right," agreed Misty. "We're dealing with a supernatural being who has lived for at least sixteen centuries. He's laid waste to cities, destroyed nations, changed history. He could have killed us all tonight instead of throwing a rock at the door. He must want something."

"See?" said Orla. "I'll be fine. Let's have dinner."

CHAPTER 15

At ten to eight the following morning, Orla freewheeled along the quayside in St Stannard to where the Stannard Hotel lurked on the edge of a salt marsh as awkwardly as a big kid at a toddler's birthday party. It was, thought Orla, an exceedingly grand building for such a tiny village: a Victorian pleasure palace of red brick and stained glass that looked like the kind of place where a genteel cocktail party might be interrupted by a murder.

To Dave, who had taken to jogging alongside the bike for exercise, the hotel looked like a trap. He paused to scratch his ears and, to be honest, catch his breath, letting Orla cycle ahead as he scanned the building. Three entrance doors and one fire escape – a green metal staircase bolted to the wall of the building – were visible, but there would be more exits on the other side. There was also a marquee set up in the courtyard: useful, thought Dave, for a soft landing in case an emergency escape from an upstairs window became necessary. He broke into a stiff-legged jog to where Orla was chaining her bike to a metal ring in the car park, a deepening sense of unease in his belly. When you'd been in the security game as long as he had, you learned to trust your instincts.

Orla glanced across the marsh to where a wall of black cloud was advancing from the North Sea, wondering if nature was sending her a warning. It was considered unlucky for witches to meet before the risen sun had passed its zenith – which was just another way of saying she should have waited until the afternoon. But there was no time for that, and she had hoped that her unexpectedly early arrival might unsettle her host. She took a deep breath, then let Dave lead her through the revolving door. With its framed maps, polished wood and deep carpets, this was exactly the place where a colonel in a cummerbund would be found dead from a single pistol shot, or a vain dowager poisoned by a crazed doctor. Except no colonels, dowagers or doctors were to be seen. Nor elegant ladies, dinner-jacketed gentlemen or white-coated waiters, because the entire property, as Uncle Valentine had said, had been rented by a short man in a black suit with painted fingernails.

Orla wiped her wellies carefully on the doormat, took a firm grip on her gwelen and let Dave take the lead. With ears four times more sensitive than a human, he heard the violin long before Orla. The target was on the first floor, so

Dave moved fast through the entrance hall, past reception, a restaurant, a bar, a library and a ballroom, until they came to the foot of a grand staircase with polished brass finials. Now Orla heard the music, fast, furious and played by a maestro.

"Up you go," she whispered.

Dave threw her a warning look. He didn't like upstairs. You could get trapped and be forced to jump from a window.

"Go," hissed Orla.

"Grrrrr," said Dave.

"Shh," said Orla.

Slowly they climbed the stairs, following the scratch and hiss of the violin until they came to a double door labelled, in gold lettering, *The Observatory*. Orla put her hand on the doorknob and gave Dave the nod: they were going in.

It was a spectacular room, furnished with deep armchairs and telescopes and with floor-to-ceiling windows looking out across the salt marsh, the magnificent view softened by a film of condensation. A short man in a black suit with a white shirt and a narrow black tie seemed to emerge from thin air, carrying a violin and a bow. He looked exactly as Uncle Valentine had described, with shiny black hair, black-lacquered fingernails and eyes as black as space.

"Sorry about the noise." He smiled, his voice a melodious Irish accent. "The violin is the Devil's instrument but it

162

keeps me out of mischief." He laid it in a red-lined case and swept a hand towards the windows. "Aren't they magnificent?" he exclaimed. "They're the only reason I picked this hotel. I've always loved drawing on glass and this is a wonderful place for making plans."

At least a dozen huge, half-molten church candles balanced on upturned wine glasses suggested he enjoyed making plans by night.

"Come in and be seated, but leave that ridiculous stick at the door," he ordered. "And the mutt. I'm allergic."

Orla looked at Dave. Dave nodded. The room, or its occupant, smelled of fresh blood. The rest of the building smelled of lavender. Orla leaned her gwelen against the wall, swallowed nervously and crossed the room.

"Godric Thorn," he said with another smile, his accent as slow and sweet as treacle. "I won't shake your hand because that could have unfortunate consequences."

"Orla Perry," replied Orla, her voice letting her down and coming out thin and weedy.

Godric threw a disapproving glance at Orla's wellies. "You could have at least taken your boots off," he said, "but I suppose you were thinking about a fast getaway." He gestured to a red velvet armchair. "Come on. Sit down and take the weight off your feet. We need to have a frank and honest discussion." He held out his hands. "Tea?"

"No thanks," said Orla, still standing.

"Thought not. You look like the straight-to-business type. We both know what we are and we both know we cannot lie. Now, please sit down."

Orla perched on the edge of the red armchair, immediately wishing she hadn't. She'd obeyed Godric. Shown weakness. She glanced at the coming storm, as though hoping it might give her a clue what to expect, but saw only the manic overlay of Godric's scribbling on the glass.

"Now then. We have a little problem, don't we, Orla?"

He had eyes like a chat show host, thought Orla: wet, black and flickering between amusement and disdain, as though she was just there to fill the gap before the commercial break.

Orla's tongue suddenly felt too big for her mouth. She coughed to clear her throat. "Not if you agree to abandon the Anna's Wood project," she replied.

Godric's eyes widened. His mouth fell open. And then he laughed, long and hard, with true delight.

"I'd heard you were astonishingly irritating, but I quite like you. How's your uncle?"

"He'll live," muttered Orla.

"I had that storm conjured up, you know," confessed Godric. "Do you know how much it costs to arrange a tempest on that scale?"

"I guessed it wasn't a natural event. So you tried to kill my uncle?"

Godric nodded. "Tried and failed." He jabbed a thumb at the windows. "The magic's right there on the glass."

"Why?" she cried. "He's just an old man."

Godric shrugged. "He told you he had his own business to attend to, but he was poking his nose into my business, making wild threats and accusations down at the GasFrac compound. I thought if he was to suffer a tragic and accidental death it would derail your investigation. Two birds with one storm, so to speak."

He certainly liked killing birds, thought Orla. "You're crazy," she retorted.

Godric raised his eyebrows and sat back in mock surprise.

"You're calling me crazy? Do you have any idea whom you're talking to?"

Orla nodded. "Godric Thorn. Knight of the Old Legion and church vandal."

"I'm not a vandal," he protested. "You know as well as I do that every church is built on our hallowed land. It seems it's only me who's interested in claiming them back. And at least I do it in a classy way. In another life I could have been a tombstone carver. I'd have enjoyed slowly chiselling the names of the dead into granite. Oh, and less of the 'Knight of the Old Legion', please." He made little quotation marks in the air. "It's pompous nonsense that the other clowns insist on. And I expect they'll continue to do so when I have them chained to walls in rat-infested oubliettes across six continents. As for me, I prefer to be known as the founder and CEO of disruptive tech think tank Thorn Corp. Like Apple, but with worms." He lowered his chin, rolled his eyes and smiled like a demon. "You can call me Godric."

"You don't scare me," said Orla bravely.

Godric wagged a finger. "No fibbing now. It's against the rules. You might pretend otherwise, but you're as terrified as Richard, little Tom and your peculiar friend Joan or whatever she calls herself."

"Leave them out of it," said Orla fiercely. "This is between you and me."

A faltering ray of sunlight brushed the windows at an angle that lit up Godric's past workings on the glass, executed in the perfect handwriting of a psychopath:

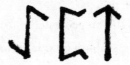

He'd drawn Eihwaz, Perthro and Tiwaz – the runes of death, destiny and battle. Orla also made out the serpent

on the staff, guardian of the east road, and the spirits of
destruction and renewal.

Below he'd scribbled some number magic in a pattern
for destruction...

9 12 22 38 44 45

26 5 3 4 21

48 16 31 8

5 11 10

13 19

1

...and an incantation of the type performed by witches
to focus the mind on a complicated or distant blasting –
although what exactly Orla couldn't guess.

NIV

EKN

KVE KNI VEK NIV EIE

INK

EVK

Godric ran his hand over his glossy hair and shook his head, like a teacher trying to decide whether to give Orla lines or a detention.

"I knew there'd be shenanigans as soon as I heard you were coming, but I suppose I'd hoped that an off-grid shack on a salt marsh surrounded by villages full of soulless morons and a complete absence of sprowl might keep you off my scent. I didn't consider that you might use that damned Coasthopper bus to reach civilisation, though." He punched his palm in irritation. "I shut down the Internet as soon as I realized that oversight, but apparently it was too late." He threw an exasperated look at Orla. "To be honest, I was so angry with you last night that my first thought was to arrange an accident involving a candle and a gas canister. But that would have been a waste of talent, and I dislike waste."

"So why are you wasting your time?" asked Orla.

"There's no sprawl under Anna's Wood."

Godric waved a dismissive hand. "That's because I blocked it. Anna's Wood is on the Treskaidekastron. But you know that already. When I get it, I'll own all thirteen points on the star; but in the meantime, I don't need sprawl leaking out like tar."

"No one can block sprawl," scoffed Orla. "It's like trying to stop the world turning."

"I can do that too." Godric smiled. "I used antimatter, if you must know. Astonishingly expensive stuff but it repels sprawl as effectively as the same poles on two magnets. The effect subsides naturally after nine full moons, but if you try and remove it before then – as I intend to do next week – it gets a bit messy."

"What do you mean?"

"There'll be an explosion. Or rather, a bioelectrical pulse. It only lasts a millisecond but it will kill everything in a three-mile radius."

Orla saw birds screaming at her to do something, then a white flash and feathers falling like snowflakes.

"So why block it?"

"Two reasons, mainly," explained Godric. "First, the pulse is quite useful. Wildlife, as you know, can be annoyingly persistent when it's struggling for survival so I prefer to wipe it all out before we start cutting trees and pouring concrete. Second, I've learned that wherever there's sprowl, there are witches who think they can fight me." He crossed his legs and brushed imaginary fluff from his trousers.

"Is it only witches who fight you?"

"Everybody fights me. Only the smart ones give up."

"Because you pay them off?"

"Because they suddenly realize that they need what I'm selling." He tilted his head. "Do you understand what I've done?"

"You've industrialized witchcraft."

Godric slapped his thigh. "Cleverer than you look! Kings, queens, prime ministers and presidents don't rule this planet. The true power is in the hands of the people who sell stuff."

"And what are you selling?" asked Orla.

"Dreams, mainly," shrugged Godric. "Having stuff isn't enough. It's the anticipation of stuff, the desire for stuff, the dreams of stuff that keeps the masses happy. Is Boxing Day better than Christmas Eve, Orla Perry?"

He raised an eyebrow. Orla scowled back.

"You get my point," smiled Godric. "Now along with GasFrac and oil companies and tech firms and film companies I own several of the biggest social media companies on earth, although I keep my name out of it.

I use them to make people want things – new phones, new homes, new cars – but imagine if you could put those advertising messages directly into the brain and make people think they thought of it themselves! You access their minds when they're sleeping, exploiting the downtime to upload the data you want them to think about. I call it BitPod – Believe in the Power of Dreams – and you don't have to download it or register to join. You just need an open mind and then I can deliver any idea I like – from a world free of injustice to, say, a shopping centre and a country park. It takes all the sprowl in the world to achieve that but it's so worth the hassle, because when you can walk through the dreams of others, Orla Perry, then you have true power."

"So you brainwash people?"

"Oh, don't start judging me," cried Godric. He straightened his tie. "I'm not just your regular crazed megalomaniac pursuing a burning desire to conquer the entire world. I'm also the original eco-warrior. The sprowl I harvest is clean and, as long as the world keeps turning, it's infinite."

He pointed a black fingernail at Orla and frowned. "You felt the pulse at Anna's Wood, didn't you? Even though the sprowl was hundreds of miles away, repelled by the antimatter, you felt it."

Orla shrugged. "Dunno."

"Don't lie," said Godric angrily.

"I'm not lying," she insisted. "I felt a weird flicker, but I didn't know it was sprowl."

"Good."

"But I think I'm allergic to it now. It hurts me."

"It's not an allergy," said Godric. "I had a curse of revulsion put on you. But even though you felt like you were poisoned, you still found and brought stored sprowl back to that filthy shack. My live feed from your kitchen has gone down, so I'm assuming you've used some of it to work up charms of protection." He flung his arms wide, grinning in admiration. "And you called me crazy! I'm truly impressed. We should work together. We should be a corporation: Thorn and Perry – no, Perry and Thorn. Imagine the wonders we could achieve!"

Orla backed away. "You put a spell on me?"

"Not me personally, obviously," protested Godric, as though affronted. "I'm not into this cottage-industry witchcraft, but when I was told it involved pricking the forehead with a poisoned thorn, it seemed delightfully apt."

He looked at Orla, awaiting her response. Orla stared back.

"Poisoned thorn," he smiled. "As in Godric Thorn."

"If you have to explain the joke, it doesn't work," replied Orla.

"Whatever," shrugged Godric. "Anyway, it's easily accomplished, but at great personal cost. Only the most desperate of witches would risk the retribution of the Rule of Threes by conjuring a curse that makes sprowl toxic to the victim."

Orla's mouth dropped open as her mind flew back to the bike crash, the long wait outside the post office and the ex-nurse turned postmistress gently removing a thorn from her face. Except that wasn't what had happened. Instead, Elizabeth Edwards had made her wait outside while she conjured the curse, then used a thorn to stab it into Orla's skin.

"I know," sighed Godric dramatically. "You can't trust anyone these days. But don't hold it against her. Elizabeth Edwards was one of those witches who refused to believe in the power of dreams, so she had to go. I gave her a choice: it could be slow, painful and lingering or, in return for a small favour, something quick. Like this." He snapped his fingers.

Orla's heart juddered and she breathed hard to quell the panic. "Have you killed the postmistress?" she gasped.

"I thought *you* killed the postmistress," countered Godric. "You persuaded her to betray me, provided me with the evidence and thus sealed her fate." He rose from his chair, crossed the room and opened a drawer. "You left this on your little tour of local witching sites."

He was holding Orla's notebook.

"Let's see…" He opened the book and flipped through the pages. "The postmistress started well: *Stop it now!* Hmm… *He hears everything* – sort of true. *You have NO IDEA who you are meddling with* – I like that one. But you were too persistent, Orla, and she went fatally off-message."

He tossed the notebook across the room and Orla caught it. He crossed to the huge picture windows overlooking the marsh. "Want to see a neat trick? Come here."

Orla went cold, then hot, the sweat running down her spine and her chest tightening. Had Godric killed the postmistress, or was he playing with her mind?

"You know that we reap what we sow," she said.

"Don't lecture me on the Rule of Threes," snapped Godric. "It's the bane of the witch's life. Every lie, every blasting, every curse, thrown back at you threefold. You give a man a headache; yours is three times worse." He glanced at Dave. "You kill a girl's best friend and three of your own die. How on earth are we supposed to get any evil done?"

"How many friends have you actually got?" asked Orla.

"None," replied Godric. "There are but two kinds of people in my world: employees and enemies. Strangers are just foes I haven't met yet."

"Is the postmistress dead?"

"Forget the postmistress," snapped Godric. "She's gone." He beckoned her to join him at the window. "You like birds, don't you?"

Orla nodded cautiously.

"Good." Godric nodded towards the marsh. "Now, if you look out there, you'll soon see a pretty grey wood pigeon flying over that ghastly swamp. It represents you, flapping feebly around trying to turn the tide."

As Orla watched, the pigeon flew into view – a bright spot in a rain-dark sky, its wings clacking as it rose and fell in the damp air. Suddenly a black blur hit it, the force of the impact scattering feathers like snowflakes as the pigeon's lifeless body dropped into the marsh.

"That was a peregrine falcon," said Godric, "playing the part of me. Do you get the point?"

"How does the Rule of Threes punish the murder of an innocent pigeon?" asked Orla.

Godric shrugged. "Minimal discomfort. A stiff neck or backache for a couple of days. Now, listen to me: I could transfer one hundred million pounds into your savings account right now." He held up a shiny black phone. "I mean, right now. You, your family and your descendants would never have to work again. Ever," he whispered. "You could be celebrities, philanthropists, conservationists – whatever you want. You could cure malaria, give hope to the poor, open a pigeon sanctuary, anything. But I don't think you'll accept that offer, will you, Orla Perry?"

Orla returned his stare, ignoring the vision of the jewel-encrusted future Godric had put inside her head. "Your black magic won't work on me."

"It's not magic," said Godric sadly. He turned back to the windows and drew a perfect pentagram in the condensation. "It's just a suggestion."

The condensation vanished when he blew on the glass but the five-pointed star was still there, as though it had been etched with a diamond.

"Shame," he said softly, as though talking to himself, "because if you're not working for me, you're my enemy."

He spun round, smiling again. "There's one more trick I'd like you to see." He placed a hand on his head as though trying to remember where he'd left his keys. "Does the mutt know of the parson's itch?" he asked.

In the doorway Dave lowered his ears, stretched his lips to show his teeth and growled like a wolf.

Orla jumped between the two. "Don't you dare hurt my dog," she cried.

"Oh, come come," protested Godric. "It's just a bit of fun." He flicked his hand and giggled. "Honestly, this one is so funny. Those afflicted with the parson's itch are pursued by an imaginary wasp – look!"

Dave's combat preparations stopped instantly. His eyes darted around the room, his attention diverted by an invisible insect.

"Stop it," hissed Orla.

"No," said Godric sharply. "And instead of worrying about trees, I urge you to focus whatever talents you have on keeping your loved ones safe. It's a very dangerous world out there, and accidents happen all the time."

The room grew suddenly cold. Godric's smile froze, and when he spoke it was as though his words were carved from ice.

"The curse of revulsion was intended to save your life, Orla Perry. Not just because I like you, but because you'd have made an unbelievably good apprentice. Instead we part as enemies in a battle only one of us can survive. Needs must. Goodbye, Orla. Don't forget your stick."

CHAPTER 16

It was raining as Orla stomped out of the hotel, pursued by Dave and an imaginary wasp.

"Stop it," she snapped as she lifted Dave into the basket. "It's all in your head."

Dave had suspected as much, but every time he looked away he could hear it buzzing behind his ears and feel the downdraught from its wings on his fur. Even the rain didn't stop it. He noticed the magpies watching from a telegraph post. Orla didn't.

Three for a girl.

Orla was both furious and terrified. Godric had never said that the postmistress was actually dead, so if she could get to the post office in Haddenham St Taylan, maybe, just maybe, she could persuade Elizabeth Edwards to climb on her yellow motorbike and ride into the sunset. The energy of pure fear carried her over the hill and down the other side, but as she sped into the village in the gathering dusk the greasy smell of smoke told her she was too late.

Two fire engines and three police cars were parked outside the dripping remains of the post office. A green plastic screen had been erected in front of the building and a young police officer was stretching blue and white tape along the privet hedge. Crepuscular Ray, unusually outdoors in daylight, was watching from beneath a broken umbrella. He looked around, startled, as Orla screeched to a breathless halt beside him.

"What happened?" she gasped.

"Post office caught fire," said Ray in his slow, low voice. He mimed an explosion with his hands. "Woof."

Dave gave him a curious look.

"Was the postmistress hurt?" asked Orla.

Ray nodded towards the smoking ruin. "They're looking for her now."

More magpies had gathered in a poplar tree to watch, and Ray gazed up at them. "Folk always blame the magpies for misfortune, but let me tell you something: those chatterpies only warn of trouble. It's the likes of you that cause it."

"I've got to go," said Orla. She turned the bike around and pedalled away, and when she was at the top of the hill, with Anna's Wood and the GasFrac compound to her left and the rain-lashed North Sea to the front, she stopped the bike and screamed.

She could only throw so much of her fright and fury into the wind. The rest stayed inside, coiled around her heart and her belly like a parasitic worm. When did apprehension become premonition? When should you ignore your fears and when should you listen to them? History books were full of stories about people overcoming their terror to accomplish astonishing feats, but they never mentioned those who had been too stupid to walk away from danger.

Should she do exactly that? She entertained the thought, allowing herself to spend sunny mornings watching black-tailed godwits fishing in the mud, biking into Wells to play pinball in the amusement arcade and eating ice cream from the shop in Cley. She'd help Tom mend his train; let Uncle Valentine teach her how to fix the outboard engine; beat Richard in a swimming race; and walk with Dave and Misty, discussing global conspiracy theories.

And she'd ignore the flashing orange lights and the clatter of the bulldozers, the groans and sighs of falling trees, and the crackle of radios as Anna's Wood was destroyed. She'd simply avoid cycling to Haddenham St Taylan again so she wouldn't have to cross the bridge and see the Swallow River all black with mud and rainbowed with spilled oil. And if anyone asked, she'd tell them that she only picked the battles she could win. Like any adult.

She turned to Dave. He was sitting on the verge, keeping

watch on the road. He looked fitter, she noticed. A bit, anyway.

"What should I do, dog?" she asked.

Dave shook himself, then wiped his face with his paws. His job was close protection, not strategic planning. In other words, it was up to Orla to get herself into situations and up to Dave to get her out of them.

"Fighting is going to hurt," mused Orla.

Fighting always hurt, thought Dave. The best soldiers – the ones who survived – always sought to avoid contact with the enemy. The imaginary wasp buzzed past like a phantom drone.

"Misty is right," said Orla softly. "We really are in trouble."

Out at sea, the red lights on the wind turbines were blinking in the twilight. Orla pushed her corkscrew hair from her eyes, wiping the rain from the scratch on her forehead where the postmistress had put a curse on her.

"We could go back to Sicow's Creek, pack a bag, grab Mala and catch the Coasthopper to King's Lynn." She grabbed Dave's head in both hands. "We could be eating toast at home by midnight, dog. What do you think?"

Dave gave a Jack Russell sneeze of frustration. The girl didn't know it but she was simply going through pre-combat checks – exhausting possibilities so she was left with inevitabilities. War with the man who smelled of blood was inevitable.

Orla kneeled in the wet grass and stared into Dave's eyes. Dave stared back. He sniffed, sneezed again, then growled.

"You're right, dog," sighed Orla. "Let's do it."

The pair were crossing the three-arched bridge over the Swallow when a sudden realization exploded in Orla's mind. She'd committed to memory the faded scrawls on Godric's window, reeling off the numbers in her head and reciting the mesmeric incantation over and over in the hope that one or the other would suddenly make sense. Suddenly one did.

INKNKEKEVEVIVININK

KEVIN

She slammed on the brakes and skidded to a halt. Dave went tactical, leaping from the basket and preparing for immediate enemy contact. When he looked back at Orla she was crouched on the bridge, rifling through her backpack. She pulled out her notebook, then a folded piece of newsprint. She looked from one to the other and back.

St Withberga
St Walstan
St Judith
Kevin D

The last words the postmistress had written. Beside the final entry, Orla's question marks. Who was this Kevin D?

She remembered the terror in the postmistress's eyes as she reached for a newspaper and tore off the front page. Bent over to protect it from the rain, Orla searched the cover for clues. The date was last week. The half-page ad was for a tyre warehouse. The banner highlighted a competition on page seven and football news on the back page. That left only the main headline:

GASFRAC WITHDRAWS
FAIR GROUND TRAVELLER SITE FUNDING

Orla looked at Dave, crouched in the grass on the far side of the bridge.

"Saddle up, dog," she called. "We've got a lead."

CHAPTER 17

"Thank God you're back," gasped Richard when Orla and Dave, one snapping at an imaginary wasp, both drenched, burst through the door. He dashed past her, down the steps and to the footbridge. "Misty, Tom," he yelled. "They're back."

Misty and Tom came running from the workshop.

"What happened?" asked Richard.

"In a moment," said Orla. "I need to see Uncle Valentine." She kicked off her wellies, dropped her sou'wester on the floor and ran up the stairs.

The old man's eyes were closed. His breathing was fast and shallow and his skin looked grey in the electric light. He'd definitely taken a turn for the worse.

"Still alive then?" he said. "What's the weather like?"

"Raining," said Orla. "Wind from the north. Uncle Valentine, I've got bad news."

Best to tell him straight, she thought, taking his hand.

It felt cold and heavy.

184

"Who died?" he asked.

"The post office burned down," said Orla. "The fire brigade are combing the wreckage for a body. Godric Thorn did it."

Uncle Valentine nodded to show he'd heard. He let out a long sigh.

"God rest her soul," he murmured.

Orla held on to his hand through a long silence, broken only by the slap of rain on the window.

Then Uncle Valentine spoke. "Will you leave me now for a bit, girl? I need to have a think."

Orla nodded. "I'll be downstairs."

"Ta," he whispered. His eyes were tightly closed but Orla saw the tear reluctantly break free and roll down his craggy cheek.

Richard, Misty and Tom were quiet as Orla relayed the news of the fire at Haddenham St Taylan. They didn't speak while Orla described her disastrous meeting with Godric Thorn and his vow to destroy anybody who got in his way, and when she explained her decision to continue the fight, you could have heard a pin drop.

"So, here's the plan," she stated. "I think we should phone an ambulance to take Uncle Valentine to hospital, and after that you should all pack your things and go."

"Go where?" asked Misty.

"Home," said Orla. "Live to fight another day and all that."

"What about you?" asked Richard.

"I've got a plan."

"What plan?" asked Misty.

Orla shrugged. "Just an idea. If it doesn't work, then I'll be straight home behind you."

Tom looked at Richard. "She's being cagey. You know what that means."

Richard nodded. "It's either extremely dangerous or extremely stupid. Or both."

"I think I'll be the judge of that," cried Orla. "Now go and pack your stuff."

Richard shook his head. "Nope."

"Nope," said Misty.

"And nope," said Tom.

"You need us," said Richard. "Otherwise you mess things up."

"I do not mess things up," protested Orla.

"You managed to get the village post office closed down," said Misty.

"Burned down, actually," noted Richard.

"And what about the brakes on the bike?" asked Tom.

"Minor hiccup."

"And how did that meeting with Godric Thorn work

out for you?" asked Richard. "Did you manage to persuade him to pack up his toys and go home?"

Orla stared at her brother. She had no answer for that.

"So we're staying," said Richard. "Not for your sake, Orla, but for the sake of the world. We can't leave its future in your hands."

"That's nice," said Orla.

"And Mr Perry stays here too," added Misty. "I agree that under normal circumstances he should be in hospital, but he's safer here behind your charms." She smiled at Orla, sweet yet menacing, like a KGB interrogator trying to be nice. "So, what's the plan, witch girl?"

Orla looked from Richard to Tom to Misty. Dave was searching for the wasp Godric had planted in his head. Maybe they'd change their minds when they realized just how dangerous and stupid her plan actually was.

"I know how Godric neutralizes anyone who disagrees with him," she said. "He gets inside their heads. Creeps into their dreams and plants ideas. They wake up and think they thought of it, that whatever he wants them to believe is their idea. That's why everyone is dreaming of shopping centres and country parks. I also know why I'm allergic to sprowl." She pointed to the scab on her forehead. "Godric told me that the postmistress put a curse of revulsion on me after I crashed the bike into her hedge. Pricked me with a rose thorn to make me ill."

"He's probably lying," sniffed Richard.

"No," said Misty. "He can't. The consequences are too destructive for a magician of his status. He's telling the truth because he has to, but how can he brainwash entire communities?"

"He needs a massive amount of sprowl to work his magic," said Orla. "He set up GasFrac to find it."

"But no single witch can achieve what he's doing," argued Misty.

"He has people working for him," said Orla. "Witches like me, conjuring his blastings and taking the impact of the Rule of Threes. The postmistress was one, and she gave me the name of someone living on a traveller site in King's Lynn. His name's Kevin D and I think he's involved so I'm going to see him tomorrow. He might be willing to talk."

"Is this the same postmistress who cursed you? Is any part of you thinking we could be walking into a trap?" asked Richard.

"You and Misty aren't coming," said Orla. "I'm taking Tom and Dave."

"Wow, thanks," said Tom. "Not."

"We're coming too," insisted Misty.

"No, you are not," argued Orla. "You're going back to

Cromer to make ten copies of that survey report. You're going to send one to the BBC, one to ITV Anglia and all but one of the others to the national newspapers. The last one you're taking to the chief planning officer and you're going to tell him or her that if those bulldozers aren't stopped, the media will want to know why. Oh, and you need to buy me a ball of red wool and some thick candles."

"You're forgetting that no one cares about your wood," said Richard. "They're too busy dreaming of a shopping centre and a country park."

"We'll make more posters," said Misty. She held up a hand as though placing the words in the air. "GasFrac has stolen your dreams."

Orla nodded. "Exactly. We'll make people suspicious of GasFrac and open their minds to an alternative future."

"Then what?" asked Richard.

"Then all I have to do is let them see the awful future the magpie showed me."

"How exactly will you do that?" asked Misty, her hands on her hips and a sceptical look on her face.

"With a blasting," said Orla. She'd just remembered something she'd seen the other day in her book of spells.

"What blasting?" pushed Misty.

"You won't have heard of it," said Orla vaguely. "It's a mindfulness thing."

"It's a Traumnebel, isn't it?"

"Might be."

"You're insane," declared Misty. "Have you any idea how much sprowl it takes to conjure a Traumnebel?"

"What's a Traumnebel?" asked Richard.

"It's a spell," said Orla. "Like YouTube for witches."

"Wow," said Tom.

"But it's loads more effective because it comes from the inside, like a vision, and not from outside, like propaganda."

"A vision?" echoed Richard.

"Oh yes." Orla nodded. "It's massively powerful."

"And massively controversial," said Misty. "Traumnebels have been used to start wars, spark persecutions and bring evil men to power. It's basically the same invasive mind control that Godric is doing."

"Exactly," said Orla. "Which is why we need to use it against him."

"I don't get it," said Tom. He had found chocolate somewhere because it was smeared on his chin.

"Traumnebel is a German word," explained Orla. "It means dream fog. You wrap a message in a spell and let it drift like mist through the night to seep into the brains of a sleeping population. Because everyone's mind is different, the dream is also slightly different for all, but the message is the same. Invade Czechoslovakia. Burn witches. Vote for el presidente. People think they've had a revelation, when in truth all that's happened is they've seen an advertisement."

Tom looked like he'd understood most of that. "Brilliant," he said. "Let's do it."

Orla shook her head. "First we speak to this guy at the traveller site. His name is Kevin D."

"No," said Tom firmly. "First I tell you my theory about the stones."

Misty sniffed the air in horror. "Has Dave farted?"

As the kids gagged and wailed, Dave strolled proudly out from under the table, wagged his tail, snapped at his wasp and farted again. It was nice to be noticed.

CHAPTER 18

The traveller site at Fair Ground was a long way from any bus stop. It was a fenced compound at the back end of a derelict industrial estate: a place of broken glass, burned-out cars and bad decisions.

Four magpies were squabbling over a discarded fried chicken box near an oily puddle, but Orla didn't notice because she was focused on the site's security.

"It doesn't look very friendly," said Tom, gazing at the caravans, the quad bikes and the open fires burning in the site.

Dave disagreed. He'd been born in a place just like this and he knew it was only as hostile as visitors made it. He'd already completed his risk assessment, identifying the big man working on a car engine as the gate guard. His backup would be in the nearest caravans. Dave tugged on the lead – his way of saying it was safe to advance – and the man looked up as the three came through the gate.

"Are you weans lost?" he growled.

"I don't think so," replied Orla. "Is this the Fair Ground Traveller Site?"

The man dropped a spanner into a box with a sharp clang. "It is," he said. "But there's no vacancies right now."

"I'm looking for Kevin D," said Orla.

The man picked up a rag, wiped his hands and then turned to face the visitors. "Never heard of him," he said. "You've got the wrong address."

"Don't think so," said Orla, staring right back at him. "I know he's here."

The man raised an eyebrow. Then he whistled. Caravan doors opened. Car bonnets shut. More huge men and a mixed bunch of dogs on ropes and chains started approaching. Dave stepped casually in front of Tom and Orla.

"And I'm telling you you're wrong," growled the man.

"Having difficulty with a couple of kids, Pat?" said one of the newcomers.

"Are any of you called Kevin D?" asked Orla. "If so, I really need your help. It's about BitPod."

"Get lost," shouted one of the men, but Pat held up his hand. "Get Mr Flaherty," he ordered.

The other dogs had got wind of a witch and were going berserk. Dave kept up a slow, friendly wag, counting the dogs. Six mutts would be a match for him if their owners set them free and he needed to decide which one to attack first. Probably the pit bull. Make an impression.

"What's all the fuss out here?" barked an irritated voice. "I'm trying to enjoy a cup of tea."

"These weans are looking for some fella called Kevin D, Mr Flaherty sir," said Pat. "I thought you should know."

A short man in his seventies came through the crowd, immaculately dressed in a tweed three-piece suit with a watch chain and a matching flat cap.

"Good morning," he said. "And who would you lot be?"

"I'm Orla Perry," said Orla. "Pleased to meet you. This is my brother Tom, and that's Dave."

"And I'm Declan Flaherty," said the short man. "Who is this Kevin D you're seeking?"

"He used to work for a man called Godric Thorn, but I believe he now lives here."

Mr Flaherty stared at Orla, long and hard, with glittering green eyes. "Do you now?" he said. Then he glanced at Tom. "That's a fine-looking terrier you've got there, lad. But he could lose a bit of weight. Will the three of you join me for a cup of tea?"

Tom fell in love with Mr Flaherty's caravan the moment he set foot in it. State-of-the-art flat-screen televisions lined one entire wall, fed by an array of satellite dishes outside.

There was enough room for two four-seater leather sofas and a dining table with eight chairs.

"Is that a dishwasher?" asked Tom.

Mr Flaherty nodded. "Aye. Sixteen settings and an eco-function. You have an eye for a well-appointed van. And that's one of the guest bathrooms through there. It's got one of those whirlpool tubs in it."

"How do you tow it?"

Mr Flaherty turned. "You don't tow a van like this, wee fella. You get a crane and you hoist it onto a sixteen-wheel low-loader and proceed to your next desired address at a safe and leisurely pace."

He took three porcelain cups and saucers, poured inky-black tea from a matching teapot and added a splash of milk.

"What are all the TVs for?" asked Orla.

"The horse racing," said the old man. "And I watch a lot of news."

Orla sipped her tea. "Have you heard the news about Anna's Wood?"

"I have," replied Mr Flaherty. "What's it to you?"

"I'm trying to stop it."

"Are you indeed?" He took a long sip of tea and looked at Dave. "Has your terrier been afflicted with the parson's itch?"

"He has," said Orla. "You know about it?"

"It's an old Romany parlour trick. They're fellow travellers along the same road." He pointed at the photographs on the wall opposite the TVs. "My ma would have known the cure. She was one of your lot. I knew what you were as soon as I saw you." He leaned forward, suddenly fierce, and Dave let out a warning growl in response.

"What's your business with our Kevin?"

"I believe that he may be able to tell me how Godric Thorn broadcasts dreams," said Orla.

"I see. But can I trust you?"

"Yes," she said firmly. "You can."

Mr Flaherty put his chin on his chest and studied Orla as though waiting to see if ill intent would show through. "All right," he said at last. "My great-grandson and -daughter will take you to him. I just hope you don't scare easily."

As if by magic – and Orla had felt a lot of that in the caravan, fizzing like sprowl used to before it hurt – there was a knock at the door.

"That'll be Isaac and Beatrice," said Mr Flaherty. "They'll look after you. You can leave the terrier here with me."

Orla felt a sudden wave of panic and threw a desperate look at Dave, who was sitting at Declan Flaherty's feet as if he had business to discuss. He gave a single wag of the tail to signal he'd be fine, and sent the girl on her way.

Long-haired and tanned from a life spent outdoors, Isaac and Beatrice were probably exactly the same age as Orla and Tom. The boy was dressed in a Red Star Belgrade football shirt; the girl was wearing a long silk dress that she held up with one hand to stop the hem dragging in the mud.

"Kevin's a strange one," said Isaac. "He never comes out of his van."

"He shouts a lot," added Beatrice. "You need to be patient with him."

"How long has he been here?" asked Orla.

"About a month, but Great-Grandad says he'll have to leave soon because it's getting too dangerous. That's his caravan there."

It stood alone in the centre of the site, surrounded by a chain-link fence topped with barbed wire, a steel gate and – Orla bent down to be sure – yes, hag stones: hundreds of them, scattered like landmines.

"Crikey," gasped Tom. "Is he a prisoner?"

Beatrice shook her head. "The fence isn't to keep him in," she said. "It's to keep the demons out."

"We're not allowed to go any further," said Isaac, "so you're on your own now. The gate code is two-one-nine-seven. It's—"

Orla smiled. "Thirteen times thirteen times thirteen."

197

Isaac smiled back. "So you're one of them too? We'd better wait here until you finish so the dogs don't kill you when you come out."

Tom laughed. No one else did. He looked at the others. "You're joking, right?"

Beatrice shook her head solemnly.

Feeling very alone and very exposed but determined not to let it show, Orla stepped confidently across the space and punched two-one-nine-seven into the lock. Inside, a small white caravan stood on a bed of white quartz, surrounded by a chain of bleached bones, sparkle jars, snakes suspended in oil, black-painted crow skulls and hundreds of crosses on chains, planted in the quartz or propped up on bricks.

"Blimey," muttered Tom.

"It's normal," said Orla.

"Actually it's not," argued Tom. "This is the height of weirdness."

"They're for protection." She'd seen it before, back in Cornwall; and in the end, none of it had worked. "Different style, but there to keep evil away."

She rapped on the door. "Kevin? It's Orla and Tom Perry. We need to talk."

"What happens if evil comes while we're in there?" whispered Tom.

Orla shook her head. "Evil usually comes at night."

That wasn't strictly true, but she needed her brother to be calm.

"Maybe he's not in," said Tom, shivering. "We should go."

The door creaked open. The sky went dark. A zombie in a banana yellow designer tracksuit with gold stripes stood in the doorway, his skin so pale and stretched Orla could almost see the nerves twitching beneath it. His bleached blond hair hung like a funeral veil around a face more bone than flesh, dark rings encircled bloodshot eyes and a silver cross hung around his neck.

"I'm Kevin Deegan," he croaked. "Is it time?"

"I'm Orla Perry," said Orla. "And it's only time to talk."

"About what?"

Orla smiled. "Better inside."

"How can I trust you?"

Orla jerked a thumb over her shoulder. "Do you think we'd have got this far if Mr Flaherty thought we were untrustworthy?"

Kevin looked at them both, wobbling slightly as though he might fall over any second. "Come in," he said. "Sorry about the mess. If I'd known you were coming..."

Mess was an understatement. Kevin's caravan made the average skip look tidy. Drink cans, crisp packets and pizza boxes littered every horizontal surface. Sticky spillages

199

coated the floor and overweight flies walked breathlessly up windows covered in greasy tinfoil. Somehow, six bright LCD screens were standing among the debris. They provided the only light.

"Have you got cockroaches?" asked Tom nervously.

Kevin shrugged. "I think the rats ate the cockroaches," he said. He jerked open a cupboard and a roll of tinfoil fell out. Catching it, he ripped off two big sheets and handed them to his visitors as though they were cushions. "Sit on these." He swung his black-rimmed eyes to Tom. "I'm joking. There are no rats or cockroaches. No living thing comes near. Except flies, and they soon drop dead."

Orla sat, squirming to remove a half-eaten kebab from beneath her. "Are you still working for Godric Thorn?" she asked.

Kevin frowned. "How old are you?"

"Thirteen."

"Why are you here?"

"To get your help. I'm going to stop the destruction of Anna's Wood."

Kevin stared hard into Orla's eyes, holding on to the wall to steady himself. Some sort of recognition flashed across his face before he switched his gaze to Tom.

"You're normal," he said. "She's not."

Tom nodded. "That's a fair appraisal."

"Is she really thirteen or is she a shape-shifter?"

"She's really thirteen."

Kevin shrugged. "I'll take your word for it. But you could be her cat."

"Are you still working for Godric Thorn?" repeated Orla, and Kevin gave a harsh laugh.

"Would I be hiding out on a traveller site if I was working for Godric Thorn? Would I be waking up every morning surprised I wasn't dead if I hadn't run away from BitPod?"

Orla didn't reply. Kevin slumped against the kitchen counter, knocking a cascade of cans and junk food wrappers on the floor. "Course I'm not working for Godric Thorn. Not any more." He ran a hand through his filthy hair.

"How old are you?" asked Tom.

"I'm seventeen next week." Kevin smiled bitterly. "Probably won't be having a party."

"Not even with the neighbours?"

Kevin laughed, short and sad. "Travellers are good people. They're like you – they know about magic – but they can't keep the Devil at bay for ever. They've given me as much protection as they can, but if we wait until his demons come there'll be deaths, so I'll be on my way soon. See how far I get."

Orla sat on the bench seat, ignoring the crackling against her back. "What went wrong, Kevin?"

He stared into the past, scratching his nose with a black fingernail. Then he swept a pizza box off the tiny dining table, carefully moved a wireless keyboard and sat down.

"I was born on a site like this, you know. In Galway. Seventh son of a seventh son and blessed with the seeing. My ma and pa made a living from me when I was a wean, taking me around the fairs and stuff, getting old ladies to ask me if I'd seen their missing sons, and young girls to enquire about their futures."

"So you were a fortune teller?" asked Tom.

"Not a fortune teller. I was – am – what they call a telepath and a seer. I can see imaginations, hear thoughts." He glanced at Orla. "Not hers, but almost anyone else's. Sometimes I get a clear view of coming events. Those who don't understand it call the seeing a gift. When I was eight, I saw what was coming to my ma and pa a week before it happened. They died in a van crash. After that, I went to live with my uncle and aunt in a house in Lancaster. They tried their best, bless them – I had my own bedroom, telly, laptop, school and all that – but it didn't work. I couldn't sit in class having my brain invaded by other people's thoughts and secrets, so I started skipping school. Hiding in my bedroom putting the old fairground tricks up online. I had 5.3 million followers by the time I was fourteen. I was KD1. *The* KD1."

"Oh my God!" gasped Tom. "I know KD1."

"Sure you do." Kevin nodded. "Everyone does. I had people from around the world asking questions, paying money." He laughed at the memory. "I know what you're thinking, Tom. I mean, I literally know what you're thinking. How did a millionaire teenage YouTube sensation end up on a traveller site in King's Lynn waiting for death to come knocking?"

He looked at Orla. "Your brother hasn't met Godric Thorn, has he? There's no picture in his mind."

"But you have," said Orla.

"He came to my uncle and aunt's house. He told them he was a specialist in the care of telepaths. He persuaded them he would invest the money for my future and get me the education I'd missed. What could they do? They were ordinary, hard-working people and he was the Devil. So they signed away my soul and I went."

"To Norfolk?"

"Eventually, after New York, LA, Rio, Buenos Aires, Sydney, Jeddah, Tel Aviv, Rome, yadda yadda yadda. Private jets and chauffeur-driven limos. All Red Bull and M&M's. Sometimes just me and a security team. Go to this restaurant and sit near those men. Take this speedboat out to that yacht and get close enough to hear their thoughts." He held out his hands. "I didn't look as stylish as this back then. I looked like nobody. The invisible man. Then this GasFrac thing started and Godric put me on the BitPod team. I wasn't just listening to thoughts any more, but stealing them. I became a dream thief." He rummaged in a fridge spotted blue with mildew. "Anyone want an energy drink?"

"No, thank you," said Orla. She stared at Kevin's silver cross.

He touched it. "This was my mum's. It's just a shape."

"I want to know how you become a dream thief," said Orla.

Kevin popped a can and took a thirsty slurp. "You've got to be born with the mental mutation. Then you've got to train it. Mind reading is predatory: you buzz around like a fly, landing on brains and sucking out the thoughts. Dream stealing is passive. You sit like a spider in the centre of a web and wait for the dreams to flutter past." He emptied the can. "Then you crush them."

"What's the point of that?" asked Tom.

"To empty people's heads so my colleagues can fill them with branded content. They use DreamCast theory and the BitPod platform to broadcast the messages we want the public to hear. Buy this. Vote for that. Believe in the power of dreams and you can have whatever we want you to think you want."

"Like shopping centres and country parks?" guessed Tom.

"You've got it," said Kevin. "We've replaced dreaming with streaming. It's nothing new. Alexander the Great used the technique in the fourth century BC, and you can be pretty sure he wasn't the first. Kings, popes, presidents and dictators have always paid magicians to cast these spells they call Traumnebels to persuade populations. BitPod is basically Traumnebel 5.0."

"Can Traumnebel 1.0 still reach these people?" asked Orla.

"Of course it can." Kevin nodded. "As long as it's performed by an expert. It's one of the hardest spells in the book."

"That's reassuring," she muttered.

"Was the pay good?" asked Tom.

Kevin shook his head. "It was beyond good. I had five million in the bank three years ago; now I have a hundred and twenty million. I have four houses I can't live in because he'll find me, and six cars I can't use to get away because I can't drive."

"So why did you stop?" asked Orla, scratching her leg.

Kevin sank onto a bench seat, sweeping debris onto the floor. "Couldn't take it any more," he said quietly. "You train so hard to maintain an open mind that you forget how to shut it down." He looked up through his yellow fringe.

"And that's when the insanity begins. Imagine a room with one hundred thousand 8K screens, beaming content every second of every minute 24/7/365. Exam rooms, missed trains, lost kittens, marshmallow castles, giant mice and falling over cliffs. Guilt, fear, and madness – I've seen things I'm glad they'll never remember when they wake up." He thumped his head with both hands. "It never stops. I had to get away."

"But if you can't tune out, where can you go?" asked Orla.

Kevin stared at her from between his bony fingers. "There aren't many options. Most dream thieves can steal from within a mile, maybe a five-mile radius. I can pick up dreams within a fifteen-mile radius. If I could escape to a place with no humans for fifteen miles in any direction, I could get some sleep."

"How do we give the people their dreams back?" she asked.

"Those I've taken, they'll never get back," sighed Kevin. "And if they're to regain the ability to dream, you need to put me out of range or shut me down."

"What about Godric?" asked Tom.

Kevin shrugged. "That's the big problem, mate. At BitPod you don't retire. You expire. When you join, you're in it for life, however long that may be." He rubbed his hair, scratched his ear and stood up, reaching inside the fridge for another energy drink. The can hissed; he swigged and sat back down. "I'm out of time. I hid in this van too long and he's found me. Those people out there won't give me up without a fight but I don't want them hurt." He nodded, as though convincing himself. "I'm out of here tonight. See how far I can run before they catch me."

"Run where?" asked Orla.

Kevin smiled. "I have a vague plan."

"I've got an idea," said Tom.

"No," said Kevin. "Absolutely not."

"You don't know what I'm going to say," protested Tom.

"Of course I do. I'm a mind reader; and no, I will not come back to Psycho's Creek with you."

"But Orla can protect you," argued Tom. "She's an actual witch, remember?"

"She can't protect me," said Kevin sadly.

He was right, thought Orla. She couldn't. Not for long, anyway. She stood up.

"Look, right now I'm all you've got, Kevin Deegan," she said. She picked up a sports bag. "We're going to fill this with hag stones and crosses and catch the last bus. And it's Sicow's Creek, by the way. Let's go."

CHAPTER 19

"Who the hell are you?" cried Misty.

Kevin looked at her, his eyelids half closed and his gaze steady. "I'm Kevin," he said. "Kevin Deegan. KD1."

"KD what?"

"KD1," said Tom. "You know, the YouTube guy."

Misty gave a blank stare.

"It's complicated," said Orla.

"It always is with you," huffed Richard. He glanced at the telepath, but didn't offer his hand. Outside, the north-westerly whistled like a psychopath.

"Kevin's life is in great danger and he has nowhere to go so we brought him here," said Orla. "How's Uncle Valentine?"

"Still sick," sighed Misty. "Presumably Kevin here is the dream thief who ran away from Godric Thorn?"

"Correct," said Orla, dumping her backpack on the kitchen table. "I bought sausages for dinner."

"Never mind dinner," protested Richard. "With him

here it could be the last supper. You've brought the enemy into our house."

"Our enemy's enemy," said Orla. "Kevin is as opposed to Godric Thorn as any of us."

"Or so he says," muttered Misty. "Have you considered for one moment that this could be a trap?"

Orla looked up at Misty, then at Richard, then back at Misty. "The thought never crossed my mind," she admitted. She turned to Kevin. "Is this a trap?" she asked.

"I don't think so."

"Oh, that's fine then," said Richard sarcastically. "Of course I haven't come to eat you, said the wolf to the piggies."

"I know what you're thinking," said Kevin.

"You have no idea," retorted Misty.

"Actually, he does," said Tom. "Seriously."

"You think I'm dressed like a thief," said Kevin. "Or a gangster, and you..." He switched his gaze to Richard, looking up through his fringe. "You think I could be violent. You're making a plan to remove the knives from..." His eyes scanned the kitchen. "That drawer."

Outside, the wind moaned, the rushes sighed and the kitchen window rattled like chattering teeth.

Kevin looked back at Misty. "You believe Orla Perry to be the most amazing human being you have ever met and you see your role as her protector and adviser. Deep in your heart you know that if bullets were flying towards her you would jump in their way. Oh, and your name isn't Misty, but you think you're a loser and you hate the one your mother gave you, so you change your identity like other people change shirts."

Misty began to blush, but Kevin continued. "You dream of being part of this family but fear you will always be an outsider. A contractor called in only when they've got themselves in trouble. That's when you're not dreaming about your poor dead dad."

"That's enough," barked Richard.

Kevin smiled and sank into a chair, drawing little spirals in the air with his forefinger. "Richard Perry. You dream of being a television presenter, a social media influencer or an actor, adored by millions, because what you crave most is approval and admiration. You worry that you're not working hard enough for any of those things to happen and that you'll end up getting a little approval and no admiration by teaching drama to bored kids. You're irritated by your brother – whom you believe to be too childish – and your sister, because you think she is more interesting than you. And even though you've already proved you can be heroic, you're scared that if the time comes again for you to step up, you won't have the courage."

"Kevin," said Orla quietly. "Stop it."

"Do me," cried Tom.

Kevin shifted his chair. "Thomas Perry. You worry that everyone is going to die and leave you all alone. The fear is based on the violence you suffered on a rainy night in Cornwall, but it has burrowed into your brain like a worm and now it's in so deep that daylight can't kill it. You don't show it, but you're terrified every time your sister leaves the house, and your dream is that the whole family stays together for ever and never leaves London again." He flicked his eyes to Misty. "You'll be delighted to know that you're part of that vision. Isn't that nice?"

He snapped his fingers at Dave. Dave ignored him. He was curled up in his basket thinking about the advice Mr Flaherty had given him when they'd sat as equals in the caravan after Orla and Tom had left. Conjure a bird to eat the wasp, he'd said, but not a crow.

"Your wee dog there has dreams too," said Kevin. "They're quite basic – lots of helicopters and kicking down doors – but he also seems to spend a large amount of time thinking about living with an old lady in a cottage next to a sausage factory in a village where nothing ever happens. As for you, Orla Perry, the window into your mind has been bricked up."

"What about *your* hopes and dreams?" wondered Misty.

Kevin looked at her. "How kind of you to ask." He pulled out his phone, holding the screen towards the others to show a photograph of a white cottage with a wet slate roof in the middle of a vast moor. His fingers touched his cross, as though in prayer. "That's one of the houses I bought. Duntieving, it's called, in Sligo on the west coast of Ireland. No neighbours for sixteen miles in any direction, and only one road in with a gate four miles from the house. I can get groceries delivered by drone and spend my time reading books about magic. It's my dream home." He flipped the phone and smiled. "And we've all got to believe in the power of dreams."

Orla glanced at Misty. "How did your day go?"

"Waste of time," confessed Misty. "Neville Clearly, the chief planning officer, refused to meet with us so we ambushed him when he left the council building to go to lunch."

"Nice work," said Orla.

Richard shook his head. "He fobbed us off. Said the decision had been made, that the courts and the Department for Environment had signed it off and he couldn't change it if he wanted to."

"He couldn't stop us putting up posters, though," added Misty. "There are a hundred and forty-four on bus stops, trees and noticeboards between here and Cromer. Plus we sent copies of that survey to the papers, the BBC and ITV Anglia, like you said." She tossed a heavy paper bag onto the table. "And I got you the wool and the candles."

"Good work," said Orla. "The posters should make minds more receptive to the Traumnebel."

"Not if Kevin there is still pinching their dreams," said Richard sourly.

"My thieving days are over," replied Kevin. "I only want to get as far away from Godric Thorn as possible."

Suddenly Dave raised his head, ears pricked up. There was trouble outside. He let out a long, low growl. Then the others heard it: the harsh rattling of a magpie very close by. Another joined in, then another, then four for a boy, five for silver, six for gold, and more. Orla pushed back her chair as Dave crept forward. She opened the door, gasped and closed it quickly.

Dave looked up at her, a puzzled growl that was part whine coming from his throat. Had Orla seen what he'd just seen?

"There's trouble coming," announced Orla. "Big trouble, I'd guess."

"Based on some birds?" asked Richard sarcastically.

"Chatterpies come to warn of trouble; it's the likes of us that cause it," said Orla softly. "That's what Crepuscular Ray said, and there are chatterpies outside now."

"How many?" asked Misty.

"All of them, I think. See for yourself."

Tom dashed to the window; Misty and Richard joined him. Orla opened the door, Dave sat at her side and Kevin behind her. The evening air was thick with magpies; hundreds, maybe thousands, were perched on posts, on rails, on the roofs and whirling through the air, their alarm calls a deafening machine-gun cacophony. And then, all at once, they left, swirling like a murmuration, their wings raising a gust that flattened the grass and sent waves along the creeks as they flew eastwards into the night.

"Wow," exclaimed Misty. "I think it's fair to say they were trying to tell us something."

"Something about Godric?" asked Tom, wide-eyed.

Orla closed the door and shot the bolt. She nodded. "I think so."

"He'll send an army of demons," said Kevin.

"Ridiculous," spluttered Richard. He stomped upstairs, muttering to himself.

"They'll steal minds and souls and perhaps even kill. It will look like a tragic accident."

Misty held up her hands. "You can stop now, Kevin. Jeez." She turned on the taps and washed her hands. "I'll cook dinner."

Orla nodded at Kevin. "We've got work to do. All-round

protection, doubled up on any east-facing points of ingress. Tom, fetch the mermaid from the smokehouse. I'm going to warn Uncle Valentine."

Uncle Valentine already knew. Sort of.

"There's trouble coming, isn't there, girl?" he croaked. He seemed even weaker than when Orla had left him that morning.

"Yep. I'm told an army of demons is coming."

"By that Irish lad?" There was clearly nothing wrong with the old man's hearing. "You think you can trust him?"

"I don't entirely know," she admitted.

Uncle Valentine gave a cynical grunt. "You invited him over my threshold. That could have been a big mistake. You mind you keep an eye on him when the fighting starts."

Orla took his hand and squeezed it. "I will," she promised.

Thirty minutes later, the curtains had been drawn and a protective ring of candles had been lit, encircling the interior of Sicow's Creek like a chain of watchtowers surrounding a fragile kingdom. Their wicks fluttered as the wind gusted outside, and the smell of sausages wafted from the kitchen to the front room, where Orla and Kevin were laying down the hag stones from the caravan.

"I may be gone when you wake," said Kevin. "I have to take my chance when I can."

"So tell me everything I need to know," demanded Orla. She was standing on a chair, stretching to hang a hag stone from the curtain rail.

"Godric's got around three hundred and fifty psychics, telepaths and witches working for him here in England, but he's got many more overseas. We can be sure all of them have been told to concentrate on this mission, so we're up against a force of around four thousand. But only one in four of those will be trying to kill us. The rest will be casting spells to protect the blasters from the Rule of Threes."

Orla stepped down from the chair and checked her stock of charms. There were just enough left – maybe – to shore up a bedroom if they needed to make a final stand upstairs. "So just a thousand trying to kill us, then. That's a relief."

"But we're quite strong here," said Kevin. "The marsh will suck the power out of any blasting, the same way water slows down bullets, and nature will be against them because they're committing evil."

Orla pulled the curtain aside and glanced out. Shreds of black cloud flew across the night sky, their bellies lit by the glare from the GasFrac compound. The moon floated like a cheese rind behind the wind-whipped trees at the back of the marsh.

She shivered. "Waning crescent," she murmured.

Kevin joined her. He smelled of sweat and kebab. "With Mercury in retrograde and Algol rising," he added. "Unluckiest planet and unluckiest star in the sky."

Orla looked at him. "You know astrology?"

"My mum did. It was her thing."

"So, is tonight a good night or a bad night for Godric to attack us?" She bent down at the fireside to give Mala a squeeze. She still hadn't dried out after the storm. Maybe it was the salt air.

"Both," said Kevin. "Blastings will be more lethal, but the comeback will be stronger. Plus, that waning crescent moon makes our protective magic much less effective." He paused, studying the fragments of the emperor's clock in their cardboard box. "A lot of Godric's workers will probably die tonight from the effects of their conjurings."

"Would he really sacrifice so many just to get you?" asked Orla.

"Dinner's ready," yelled Misty.

Kevin gazed at her sadly. "Not to get me, Orla. He can take me any time. This is all for you."

CHAPTER 20

As Orla, Misty, Kevin and Tom ate their dinner – all agreed that sausages, beans and mash was quite simply the finest meal on earth – Dave padded around the house, his claws clicking on the floorboards as he checked windows and lowered his nose to sniff what was coming under the doors. Sicow's Creek felt different tonight, as though it had searchlights trained on it or had been laser-marked for an air strike. With an attack imminent, Dave needed to check the entries and exits and double-check the escape routes and rendezvous points. And he needed everyone in one place.

He put his nose around the door of Uncle Valentine's room. Survival meant sticking together, and since they couldn't move the old man from his bed, they'd have to mount their defence from his room. Dave crept along the landing, staying close to the wall and using his nose to press open the door to Greylag, where Richard was lying on his bed, staring miserably at the ceiling. He checked Coot and Nightjar, then sat down at the top of the stairs, sniffed his bum, scratched his ear and sighed. Staying in the old man's room meant not only surrendering the ground floor without a fight, but also that escape would have to be through the windows.

Somewhere near by, an imaginary wasp hovered and Dave sent an imaginary woodpecker after it. He jogged downstairs and across the damp Afghan rug, then leapt with cat-like grace onto the draining board, sending two saucepans and a potato masher crashing to the floor. Collateral damage, he thought, as three out of the four kids at the table jumped out of their skin.

"Get down, Dave," scolded Orla.

Then the lights went out.

For a moment in the candlelight, nobody said a word. Then Misty murmured, "Oops."

Richard came thumping down the stairs.

"Has the generator gone out?" he asked.

"Not by accident," said Kevin. "You'd better have some food before it all starts."

"No," retorted Richard angrily, putting on one of Uncle Valentine's coats. "I actually think I'd better go and check the generator."

"Don't be mad," said Misty.

"The wind has dropped," observed Tom. "It's gone quiet out there."

"Good," said Richard, fumbling for the torch app on his phone.

Orla stood up. "Do not go out there, Richard."

"Or what?" he replied, pulling open the back door. He stood on the threshold, dead still. "Oh. My. Days," he gasped. "Look at this."

Orla rushed to the door. Outside, maybe two miles away, a fiery streak was zigzagging across the marsh. The GasFrac compound had gone dark and the orange line had turned the night ablaze, its flare reflected as it zipped past pools and channels.

"Drat," muttered Orla, running to the front room window. "It's following the dyke paths." She was going to need sprowl.

"What is it?" asked Richard.

"It's show time, mate," said Kevin. "Salt water sucks the power out of any blasting and that's what's slowing it down and causing the orange streak. It's like the tail of a meteorite punching through the atmosphere, but the drag isn't enough to stop it hitting us like a wrecking ball."

Dave darted to the back door, pushing past Richard to get a better view. Ninety seconds until impact, he guessed. Or less. He ran halfway up the stairs and barked three times, loud and clear. Orla got it.

"Grab the candles and follow Dave," she yelled, seizing

her backpack. "He knows what he's doing. And Tom, bring the mermaid."

They all followed the Jack Russell into Uncle Valentine's room and slammed the door. Orla tipped out the last seven hag stones from Kevin's expensive sports bag, laid them across the door and hung three of the heaviest crosses from the handle.

"Can I do anything to help?" asked Uncle Valentine from his bed. He didn't sound particularly scared.

Orla smiled. "No, thank you, Uncle." She grabbed the witch jars, placing two on the floor with the hag stones and one on the windowsill. Outside the house, the wind had risen and as Misty and Richard fumbled to relight the candles, the fierce orange light of the streak of fire flickered behind the curtains. A sudden scream, long and agonized, pierced the night. Then another. And another.

"Don't put it there," said Kevin, moving the jar of nails from the windowsill. "When that window gets blown in, we'll be picking those nails out of our faces." He placed it on the floor.

"He's conjured a storm," said Orla.

"No, he hasn't," argued Kevin. "Nature is against him. The wind is on our side."

"So what's the howling?" asked Misty.

Kevin stared at her. "I thought only one in four of

Godric's witches would be blasting us while the others protected them, but I was wrong. He must have put the full four thousand against us."

"I don't follow you," said Misty.

"He's conjuring up a Korsanum. That takes a massive amount of psychic energy."

A screech so loud it seemed to bend the walls hit the room like a bomb blast, blowing out the candles as the fire approached, roaring like a rocket.

"A what?" asked Richard.

"Korsanum," said Misty. "It's an Armenian term. Means ruination. The Zoroastrian magicians called it Tabahi, or total destruction."

"The Korsanum uses human energy," said Kevin. "It calls on the souls of all who sold out to Godric Thorn, dead or alive. They have no choice but to heed that call."

Richard was sat next to Misty, his knees pulled up to his chest. "Tell me one thing," he said. "Is this situation actually survivable?"

"Oh my God," gasped Tom. An intense blue light was thrusting up between the floorboards. "Downstairs is on fire."

"It's not fire," said Misty. "It's earthquake light."

"Earthquake light?" asked Tom.

"Google it," she snapped.

Kevin stood up to look out of the window. "But the real fire—"

He didn't finish. A flash burst the glass and threw him across the room. He landed wide-eyed and breathless, his white hands touching a face streaked with blood.

"I'm OK," he gasped. "I'm—"

The screams came back to drown him out, howling like dive-bombers, like sirens, like a runaway train as the blue light shot through the walls and the floors like laser beams. Floorboards creaked. The door bowed inwards, cracks splintering the panels. Kevin crawled back to the group, huddled and holding hands at the side of Uncle Valentine's bed.

"You asked if we'd survive until tomorrow, Richard," he said, shouting to make himself heard. "The answer is that I honestly don't know. I can't see any future beyond tonight."

A crash came from downstairs and Dave sprinted to the door, his hackles up and his nose down. Whatever they were, they were inside the house. And soon they'd be coming up the stairs.

"They're demons," said Kevin. "If you look at them, they'll steal your mind. Then they'll take your soul. So keep your eyes shut."

"But remember that they exist only in our minds," said

Orla. She gripped Tom's shoulder and looked at Richard, then Misty. "They're not really here. You understand? They're only as real as you want to make them."

Kevin pointed at the door. "When they break through, you get on your knees, put your head on the floor and cover your ears with your hands. Whatever they do or say, whatever they make you think, do not look up." He glanced at Uncle Valentine. "Kevin Deegan, sir. Delighted to meet you. Would you pull the blankets up over your head and keep them there until tomorrow?"

Uncle Valentine rolled his eyes, but did as he was told.

"What can we do?" gasped Misty. "Orla! What can we do?"

Orla reached into her backpack for her spell book and for Mala, then went cold. Mala was downstairs, by the hearth. She might as well have been in Madrid. Something heavy smashed against the door. Something else crashed into the roof. The curtains were beginning to smoulder. She needed a charm. Something that would save lives. Something to deliver them from evil. Something buried so deep in her DNA that even the Devil himself couldn't reach in and seize it. Her hand went to her throat, gripping the silver star she wore around her neck, and then she found it.

"A banishing pentagram," she cried. "Give me the mermaid, Tom."

Tom's mouth sagged open, his crumbling face saying more than words ever could.

Orla's heart sank. "You didn't fetch it, did you?"

"I forgot," murmured Tom. He looked like he was going to cry.

"Is she in the kitchen?" asked Orla.

"She's still in the smokehouse," he mumbled. Tears were rolling down his face now.

"In the smokehouse?" exclaimed Orla, incredulous. "You mean outside, in the dark, in the witching shed?" She closed her eyes.

"What now?" cried Richard.

A nail shot out of a floorboard, embedding itself in the ceiling. Then another, sending a cascade of plaster dust drifting through the strobing blue light.

Tom stood up. "I'll go and fetch it."

"No, you will not," growled Orla. She took a deep breath, opened her eyes and pulled Dave's tactical harness from her backpack.

"Dog?" she said.

Dave padded over to be clipped in. Orla dug her bandana from her pocket, still pungent with serpent smoke, and held it out for Dave to sniff.

He didn't need to. He already understood the mission.

"Ready?" she whispered. "Keep your eyes shut as tight as you can, dog, and fetch the mermaid."

Dave nodded and closed his eyes. He felt Orla's hand close around the handle on his harness, heard the door creak open, and was suddenly hurled into a world of pain.

CHAPTER 21

It felt like a wind tunnel full of flying glass. Or the shrapnel blast from a car bomb. And the noise, thought Dave, was enough to turn his brain to jelly. Buffeted from side to side as though by stampeding cattle, he sprinted to the stairs, eyes still tightly shut, and turned right. It was just thirteen steps to the bottom, but as he began his descent, something with claws like a leopard grabbed his throat, choking and pushing him back. Dave recoiled, and the death grip tightened. He snapped blindly, then, as he felt teeth closing around his spine, he dropped a shoulder and rolled, breaking free.

He cleared the stairs in three jumps, but there was more trouble waiting at the bottom. Things that felt like bats, winged and screechy, were targeting his face. They were trying to peel open his eyes and steal his mind.

He grabbed one out of the air, shook it until it snapped then spat it out. Three more took its place, their fangs tearing at his ears and lips. He shook them off, biting the life from them, but still more attacked, and he was already weakening.

Suddenly the frenzy abated and, resisting the almost overwhelming urge to open his eyes, Dave dropped to his belly to assess the situation. Whatever creatures had been launching the air attacks were still whirling furiously around him, but something was holding the needle-toothed screechers back. Dave squirmed, his nose twitching. His tummy was wet. He licked the floor and tasted salt. But he wasn't on the floor. He was on Uncle Valentine's Afghan rug – the same rug that had yet to dry out after the old man had lain upon it, all soaked with seawater.

Dave rolled off the rug and instantly the screechers attacked. He rolled back and they withdrew. They clearly couldn't operate in or around salt water. The Jack Russell's tail thumped twice in glee, and then he exploded into a sprint, following his nose through the house, out of the back door, down the steps and onto the jetty, pursued by seething furies. He didn't see where the jetty ended because his eyes were still closed and he landed in the creek like a bag of cement. Dog-paddling – obviously – Dave headed towards the sea, the screechers whirling along the bank beside him.

A hundred yards or so along there was a culvert leading through the dyke that he had noticed during a daytime reconnaissance patrol. It led to a tidal channel that dog-legged back towards Sicow's Creek, passing the smokehouse on its third turn. This was the kind of attention to detail, Dave reminded himself, that separated the professionals from the amateurs.

Feeling with a front paw and steering with his tail, he found the opening and swam inside, treading water for a second to catch his breath. There was a short moment on the other side before the swarm picked up his trail, giving Dave the opportunity to open his eyes and look around. The marsh was veiled in a spooky blue mist and everything had gone suspiciously quiet. It was, felt Dave, too quiet, like the strange silence before an ambush. Staying in the water was the safest option but there was no time left for that. He had to employ four-paw drive and go overland, moving fast and low, sticking to the shadows and hoping that the seawater and marsh slime in his coat would offer protection.

He reached the smokehouse undetected, crept up the steps, shoulder-barged the door and slipped inside, nose twitching. He could smell the strange and pungent odour of the protective oils enveloping the mermaid coming from somewhere near the workbench. He hopped onto the bench to get a better sniff.

And came face to face with a demon.

It was like an ugly old woman no bigger than a rat dressed in baggy black leather with a shiny red face and glittering eyes. It was sat on its haunches on the bench, its oversized wings hanging loosely and dripping with foul-smelling sweat. Its expression, noted Dave, was one of derision and superiority – it was watching to see his reaction as it stole his mind. Fighting against the sensation that he was falling, Dave focused on the face. It was familiar: the plump features of someone he'd recently met. Someone who'd taken an instant dislike to him. Someone who was now sucking the sanity from his brain with a smile of smug self-satisfaction. Then he got it: it was Jemima Water-Mills. She'd sold her soul to Godric Thorn and was now part of the demon cohort.

"Aww. Was that an ickle spark of doggy recognition?" she asked in a little girl voice, her head tilted to one side. "How sweet. When I've finished with you, I'm going to pop back to that shockingly decorated shack, find that awful child you hang around with and cancel her. But first, you smelly mongrel, I need to take your soul. Come to Jem—"

Dave lunged before she could finish. His jaws snapped as though catching a wasp and he swallowed the demon like a thrown sausage. She tasted quite artificial, but now, he figured, he had his mind back. He belched, then ran his nose along each row of drawers until he found the one containing the mermaid. Seconds later, she was safe in his custody, like a rescued hostage. He paused by the door to look across the marsh to Sicow's Creek, which was expanding and shrinking as though gasping for breath – and smouldering like the last inch of the fuse on a high-explosive bomb. Dave guessed he had maybe two minutes. After that, it would be too late. He grabbed the bundle, closed his eyes and sprinted for home.

Meanwhile, Orla had a problem. As boards popped and splintered, and the others were beating out the fire on the curtains and pushing furniture up against the door, she'd drawn her banishing pentagram. It was the most elementary witchcraft: a five-pointed star correctly aligned, with a pentagon in the middle formed by the line. If you got the magic right, anyone within that pentagon would be protected from blastings as if they were stood within a wall of reinforced, lead-lined concrete. But not for ever. A banishing pentagram was powered by sprowl, and would only shield against evil for as long as that sprowl lasted. The ideal, according to Orla's spell book, was a three to one ratio, meaning that you needed three times as much sprowl as that used by your enemy to ensure that you'd come to no harm. But Uncle Valentine's bedroom was too small to draw a pentagram big enough to protect six humans and one dog.

And where was that dog? Deep down, Orla knew Dave had maybe a ten per cent chance of surviving the mission, but she'd swallowed the guilt and the fear because if Dave failed, then no one would survive. And even if he succeeded in fetching the sprowl, there was no guarantee that there would be enough of it to protect them against this horror. But she couldn't let anyone else know that.

"You really believe you can beat this, don't you?" said Kevin.

"Yep," said Orla, dragging her chalk across the boards.

He laughed. "You know what's out there, don't you?"

"Lost souls," retorted Orla.

"Sold souls, actually. I always wondered what it meant to sell your soul to the Devil, and now I know. You incur a debt that one day will have to be repaid. I did it. I took the money, the cars, the superstar lifestyle and the amazing clothes..."

Orla looked at his stained yellow tracksuit. "Amazing clothes? Really?"

"Very funny," sniffed Kevin. "This is Versace. You realize that my soul is probably one of those out there, leading them in?"

"It's all in the mind," Orla said firmly.

An electric blue streak, like a bolt of lightning, blazed through the broken window, showering Uncle Valentine's bed with broken glass and bouncing off the opposite wall in a cascade of white sparks.

"Really?" asked Kevin.

"Block that window," yelled Misty, her face streaked with blood.

"Do not touch anything that wasn't in this room before the attack," shouted Kevin. "Everything else will be tainted with evil. After you get through the night, only Orla will be able to touch what's left."

"*If* we get through the night," muttered Richard. "Kevin, help me move the wardrobe in front of the window."

"The hag stones are burning," warned Tom. "And the nails are glowing."

A floorboard suddenly sprang from the joists, splinters flying like shrapnel. A witch jar shattered, spilling red-hot nails over the floor. As Richard poured herbal tea on them to prevent a fire, Orla stared at her pentagram. It was too small.

"Let's get Uncle Valentine out of bed," she ordered. "We need him inside this shape."

A violent thudding at the door sent a chill through the room.

"That's it," said Kevin. "They're wearing down the stones."

"So get in the pentagram," barked Orla. "Now!"

The thudding grew louder and more persistent as, one by one, like dying candles, the hag stones flared and went out.

"This is it," said Richard. "Get ready."

"Hold on a sec," said Orla. "Evil souls don't knock."

She skirted the stones, barged a chest of drawers aside and, shielding her eyes, opened the door. Dave burst in with not one but two rescued hostages: the mermaid and Mala too.

"Good dog," she cried, slamming the door. "Push that chest back."

"He's covered in ectoplasm," gasped Richard.

Orla lifted Dave, sniffing his coat. "It's just creek slime," she said, hugging him to her chest. "Now get Uncle Valentine upright so we can all prop him up in the middle. And don't step over the line, because that breaks the charm."

A sound like a crashing jet was coming closer and closer: the noise of speed, rage and impending doom.

"There's not enough room," said Misty.

"There is," insisted Orla. She had Dave under one arm, Mala under the other and the mermaid gripped in both hands. She could feel the sprowl cracking her knuckles, thumping her arms and rushing through her body like snake venom but she would not release it until the demons smashed through the door. "Face outwards, link arms and squeeze tight."

"It's impossible," cried Richard. "There are too many of us."

"We've no choice," growled Orla. "Squeeze in tighter. We need to be inside the line."

"I know what happens next," said Kevin. He shrugged himself free from the group and stepped outside the pentagram. "It would never have worked, Orla." He smiled sadly. "A pentagram cannot protect more people than its points. That's five. Not six. And I think you know that." He gave Dave a scratch behind a slimy ear. "Keep her safe, mate."

"Get back in here," demanded Orla.

Kevin shook his head. "No room. And anyway, I've just remembered I left my phone downstairs." He shoved the chest of drawers aside and turned, one hand on the door handle, the other gripping his cross. It was much more than just a shape now.

"Close your eyes, kids." He smiled again. "Sweet dreams."

He opened the door, and all hell blew in.

CHAPTER 22

They came close – so close Orla could feel the fetid air from their wings as they screeched furiously past – but the mermaid's power kept them outside the pentagram. Outside, the wind moaned and the unquiet souls summoned to Sicow's Creek raged against it, but with less and less force. The attack had peaked and the stored sprowl in the mermaid had outlasted all the forces of evil. By dawn it was over, and the carved mermaid had turned to dust.

They'd had all night, arms linked around Uncle Valentine like martyrs on the stake, eyes tight shut, to ponder Kevin's fate. Knowing that he'd never make it to his house in Ireland, had he sacrificed himself to save his new friends? Or had he left the house with a free pass from Godric Thorn?

"He was a traitor," muttered Richard. He was sitting on the top stair amid a confetti of shredded wallpaper. "An enemy agent inside our house."

Misty was sat on the next stair down. "I prefer to think hero," she said quietly.

"I liked him," said Tom, emerging from his bedroom. He was in shock, his hair standing on end and his eyes ringed with red circles. His bed had been snapped in two like a custard cream, his bedroom door punched off its hinges.

Orla limped out from Uncle Valentine's bedroom dragging a bin bag. "I've swept up the glass and the nails," she said. "It's heavily contaminated so don't touch anything. I'll have to dispose of it far out at sea."

"How's UV?" asked Tom.

"Really weak," sighed Orla. "He should be in hospital, but Misty is right. We won't be able to protect him there."

"We need to look for Kevin," said Misty.

"We do," agreed Orla. "But first we all need to swim in the creek. Get right under the salt water to wash off any trace of last night."

With Dave on point, they stumbled into a cloudless April dawn in swimsuits, looking for all the world like four kids and a dog on holiday. Orla walked to the end of the jetty and jumped straight in. Misty followed. Richard and Tom made a bit more of a fuss about it, climbing gingerly down the ladder and shrieking as Orla and Misty splashed them. At last, all were submerged and then Misty turned to look back.

"Oh my God," she breathed. "Look at the house."

Sicow's Creek looked like it had been hit by a hurricane, with every window broken and roof slates scattered across the marsh. The weatherboard walls were charred up to the lower window frames and yet the fire had never properly taken hold. Why not? wondered Orla. Had the charms really worked that well? She was drying herself with a scratchy old towel, watching Tom wading along the edge of the channel. She glanced right, to where Dave was guarding the bridge, and when she looked back, Tom was calling her.

"Come quick," he yelled. "I've found Kevin's shoe."

Or what was left of the shoe. The Gucci label was half visible but the rest was a molten ball of rubber and plastic. Close by, a glint in the mud. It was silver; the twisted lump of metal had melted and then solidified. The chain was still attached. Tom picked it up. "It's his cross," he mumbled.

Misty took it from him and showed it to Richard.

"Hero," she snapped as she walked past him and into the house.

Orla wrapped herself in her towel and walked down the path towards the beach. She stopped when she was alone, hugging herself against a chill that came more from within than from the wind. She needed a little time to gather her thoughts. A month would have been about right. She got two minutes.

"What now?" asked Richard. He was shivering in the breeze.

What now indeed, thought Orla, staring seawards. With Kevin missing, presumed dead, there would be no more stolen dreams. Minds were free, which would make them more receptive to a Traumnebel. It was the best possible outcome from a terrible night, but for one flaw.

"I think it's over," she said. "We're out of sprowl and I can't gather any more until this spell wears off."

"How long will that take?"

"A moon cycle. Twenty-eight days."

"We can't wait that long," said Richard. "Isn't there some kind of antidote?"

"There's a charm for the lifting of curses but it has to be conjured by another witch," explained Orla. "Know any?"

"So we should cut and run. If those demons come again, we won't survive."

Orla nodded. He was probably right. The graveyards were full of those who didn't know when to give up.

"What's the plan?" called Misty, emerging from the broken house. She was dressed in a beige safari suit and a yellow roll-neck jumper. Richard looked at Orla and raised his eyebrows in horror.

"We're out of sprowl and Orla's cursed so the Traumthing is off," he told her. "We're going to quit while we're ahead."

Misty put her hands on her hips and gave Orla a hard stare. "Is this your plan or his?"

Orla sighed. "It's Friday morning. The bulldozers will be in Anna's Wood on Monday. Do you know where I can find a ton of sprowl by then? Because that's the only way we can defeat them."

Misty shook her head. She turned and walked back into the house.

"So I guess we're out of here, then?" said Richard hopefully.

Dave trotted past, snapping half-heartedly at his wasp. His imaginary woodpecker was actually more annoying.

"It's a beautiful day," said Orla, gazing down the path to a beach she had yet to visit and pondering an end she couldn't accept. She couldn't just give up. There had to be a way.

"Don't change the subject," grumbled Richard. "Are we out of here or not?"

Dave was barking at the sky.

Richard turned. "I'll go and check the Coasthopper timetable. Start packing."

Dave was still barking at the sky, and now Tom was yelling.

Something about a cat.

A cat on the roof.

Orla looked to where Tom was pointing at an orange blob.

"Fetch the ladders," she cried. "It's Vinegar Tom."

CHAPTER 23

The cat sat on the mat in the middle of the kitchen table. The four kids surrounded it, gazing in wonder at its moth-eaten coat and yellow glass eyes. Dave was on the doorstep: partly because he was on guard duty and partly on account of the astonishingly noxious emissions from his bum. The dark soul of Jemima Water-Mills was wreaking a pungent revenge.

Vinegar Tom had a red ribbon around his neck with a leather pouch attached. Carefully Orla untied the ribbon and opened the pouch. Inside was a folded letter, written in neat script with a fountain pen. Orla read it out.

Dear Miss Perry,

I am taking my leave of the village. It is not a decision I make lightly but rather one based on the growing realization that it is better to live for a just cause than to die for a lost one. Or a wicked one.

Your clumsy arrival and subsequent insistence on meddling in local affairs has only hastened that decision, and so Post Office Counter services in Haddenham St Taylan are henceforth suspended until a suitable replacement is appointed.

You will in time learn that I hindered your efforts to fight our common enemy. I did so out of fear for my own life, but that is no excuse and I sincerely apologize for this act of unforgivable selfishness and cowardice.

I politely request that you and your uncle do not try to make further contact with me as I think maintaining a safe distance is beneficial to all. In return, I leave you Vinegar Tom. He is rather bedraggled, but he has huge inner strength.

Yours in haste,

Elizabeth Edwards

"Wow," said Orla, folding the letter and catching her breath as a wave of relief left her giddy and weak-kneed. The postmistress was alive.

"What a weird leaving present," marvelled Tom. He poked Vinegar Tom with a finger, then recoiled as though scratched. "Ow!"

"Better show that cat some respect," warned Orla. She held out her hand, feeling her fingernails throbbing, her knuckles aching and shooting pains running up her arm. "Vinegar Tom's inner strength is super-concentrated sprowl." She glanced at the others, fighting against the desire to dance on the table with joy. Things were looking up. "If you're up for it, we'll have a Traumnebel after all."

"Right," announced Misty. "I need to get changed."

Orla followed her upstairs to fetch her book of spells from its hiding place. When she returned, Richard and Tom were arguing over how Vinegar Tom had ended up on the top of the chimney. Dave was in the doorway, staring suspiciously at the cat.

"Can witches actually fly?" asked Tom.

Orla shook her head. "Nope."

"So how did the cat get up there?"

"Good question," she said.

Heavy footsteps thumped on the stairs as a warrior descended in black boots, black combat trousers, a black T-shirt and a black leather biker jacket, her black hair half hidden beneath a black commando beanie.

"Blimey!" gasped Richard. "What's happened to you?"

"Misty wasn't cut out for combat operations," said Misty. "So Raven has flown in to take her place."

"Back in black," noted Richard. "Lovely to see you again."

Orla puffed out her cheeks and shook her head. "This is so confusing," she sighed.

Raven screwed up her face; Richard did likewise. Dave had just farted.

"Jesus!" wheezed Richard. "That dog's eaten something truly evil."

Dave crept away. There was more truth to that than anyone realized.

"I need to perform that Traumnebel in Anna's Wood tonight," said Orla. "The moon is all wrong but we have no choice."

"You what?" spluttered Richard. "Why in the wood? Do it in the smokehouse, for goodness' sake."

Orla shook her head. "Can't."

"She's right," said Raven. "If the Traumnebel has a geographical objective, it must be cast from that objective. Haven't you read *Malleus Maleficarum*?"

Richard rolled his eyes. "Of course I flipping haven't."

Orla waved her book of spells in the air. "I need to fetch stuff. Loads of stuff. What are you lot going to do?"

"Put up more posters," decided Richard. "Anything to make more people receptive."

"Stay here, fix up the house and keep watch on UV," said Tom.

"Infiltrate the GasFrac compound and sabotage the bulldozers," declared Raven.

"I preferred you as Misty," said Richard.

"Take Dave with you," ordered Orla. "And don't get caught."

CHAPTER 24

Orla sat on a chair beside Uncle Valentine's bed and opened her book of spells. There were three variations on the Traumnebel theme, and while all involved the usual rite of purification and declarations of good intention, the rituals and the ingredients necessary to make them work were all quite different. Which was annoying, because Orla had one shot at getting this spell right and neither the wisdom nor the experience to make an educated guess at which version was most likely to succeed.

She studied the first set of instructions, recorded by twelve-year-old Miss Lamorna Teague on 21 November 2005, the neat handwriting listing the ingredients: camphor, oil of mercury, dust from a west-side grave, burned owl feathers and more, then the ritual and then the process, where the words *ALLOW THREE HOURS* were double underlined.

Orla flipped forward to a page inscribed *Boskerry, 5 April 2008*. Underneath, sketches, lists and instructions entitled "How to Revive a Cat". As she read it, Orla realized with a shudder that it was the spell she had used last summer to bring Dave back to life. She flicked forward to *Samhain, Porthzennor 2009*. The handwriting had lost its neatness, and the characters were leaning backwards. Orla could imagine the young witch sitting on the sidelines at Samhain – the pagan autumn festival – scribbling down the words of an old peller and not noticing how her life was sliding into a shadowland of secrets and threats. Was that where Orla was heading too, afflicted by a curse that attracted trouble like wasps? Would she be forced to push friends and family away in order to protect them, doomed by her so-called gift to a life of fear and isolation? Or was it her own stupid fault for meddling in matters that didn't concern her and narrowly avoiding getting everyone killed?

Or almost everyone. She glanced at what remained of the chalk pentagram that would never have protected six and dropped a hand to trace the outline.

"Thank you, Kevin," she whispered.

Suddenly Uncle Valentine, who until this moment had been deathly silent, let out a snore that sounded like a pig being kicked up the bum. Then another. Orla stood up and sighed. She couldn't work in here, so she went downstairs and out to the jetty where the sandpipers, the godwits and the curlews were quietly working in the low tide mud. She needed to analyse all three sets of instructions in detail in order to guess which one worked best, and she needed to do it fast.

As she opened the book, a breeze rolled up the creek, leaving ripples on the slack water. It hit the spell book as though aiming for it, but gently, with just enough strength to riffle the pages. The book stayed open on the third Traumnebel, dated *Imbolc 2014* – the February feast of St Brigid and a celebration of the coming end of winter's oppression.

Orla raised an eyebrow. "Really?" she said to the wind. "Prove it." She laid the closed book on the jetty and took a step backwards. As though accepting the challenge, the breeze returned and reopened the book at *Imbolc*.

"One more time. Just to be sure."

The wind complied.

"OK," said Orla. "Thanks. I'll make a list."

Much of what she required was in the smokehouse – the witching shed – but she needed certain fresh botanicals and didn't have the time to waste searching. So she ran back to the house, grabbed the rum bottle, charged up the stairs, flopped down on Uncle Valentine's bed and poked him.

"Wake up!" she cried. "Your help is needed in an important project."

Uncle Valentine grunted, so she shook him again. "Waaaake uuuup. Wakey-wakey. Wakey-wakey wakey-wa—"

"What the bloomin' heck's got into you?" he roared.

"Need your help," said Orla, pouring a tot of rum and passing it over. "Ingredients for a spell."

"That's a sparrow's toast," he spluttered. "What do you want to know?"

"Where can I get mugwort?"

"Jack bacca is what we call it round here," coughed Uncle Valentine. "Look in the copse behind the marsh."

"Valerian?"

"Sunny side of the lane up Gallows Hill."

"Good," said Orla. "Dust from a roadside grave?"

Uncle Valentine shifted himself to get a better look at his great-niece. "Does your mother know what you get up to on your holidays?" he asked.

"Nope. Roadside grave?"

"Will a crossroads do?"

Orla nodded. "That's even better."

"Right you are. There's a smuggler's grave marked by a green rock up behind St Stannard by the Maltleck ford." He took a long slug of rum. "He was a Dutchman."

"Noted," said Orla. "Quicksilver?"

"If there's none in the smokehouse, there'll be some in

the rope-house. It's in a jar on the middle shelf next to the distress flares. Use both hands getting it down because it's damned heavy."

"Excellent," said Orla, leaning across to peck Uncle Valentine on the cheek. "I'll take that," she announced with a smile, snatching the rum bottle.

She fetched the quicksilver from the extremely heavy jar in the rope-house and shoved three distress flares into her backpack. She found Tom forlornly looking for more signs of Kevin, told him to check on Uncle Valentine every thirty minutes, and then pedalled away from Sicow's Creek. It was a little after 10.30 a.m., and even though it was a sunny April day, she felt desperately unsafe, especially without Dave in the basket. Today, though, Raven needed his special skills more.

By 2 p.m. she had everything on the list and was cycling back along the coast road, wondering why it had been so easy. It was as though the horror of last night had never happened and this beautiful day, with sunshine's promise of summer, was the only reality. Where was Godric's second wave? Where was the latent chill of menace? All seemed at peace in Norfolk apart from the police car racing along the coast road, sirens blaring, lights flashing and an angry prisoner with a muddy, sullen-looking dog in the back.

Orla slammed on the brakes. Had Raven and Dave been arrested? She felt a rush of worry. Although, frankly, they were safer locked up in a cell. But maybe it wasn't them. Maybe it was a completely different black-clad eco-warrior and her Jack Russell being carted off to a police station.

As soon as she got back to Sicow's Creek she asked Tom if he'd heard anything, but he had other matters on his mind.

"You need to see this," he said, striding back along the dyke towards the road.

"Have you at least heard from them?" asked Orla, jogging to catch up.

"Nope."

"Did you hear a police siren?"

"Nope," he repeated. "Now, look at this." He was pointing at a gorse bush.

"And?"

"Look behind."

"Tyre tracks," she noted.

"Motorbike tyre tracks," he corrected. "And who do we know who rides a motorbike?"

"The postmistress?" guessed Orla.

"Correct," said Tom. "Now how do you explain this?"

He was pointing into the ditch where, floating in the brackish water, was a broom. A broom straight out of a fairy tale. The kind of broom that witches fly on in picture books.

Orla had no words. "I, er, um..." she stammered.

"You said witches can't fly," said Tom. "I say they can. She used it to fly up to the chimney and leave her dead cat."

"But why did she leave her broom behind?" asked Orla.

"Because," said Tom triumphantly, "she's turned her back on witchcraft and has decided to live an honest life."

"Witchcraft isn't a criminal activity," argued Orla, and Tom gave her a long, hard look.

"Really?" he said. "So what went on last night was all legal and totally above board?" He stomped off, too angry to wait for an answer, then stopped. "And another thing, Orla Perry."

"What?"

"These." Tom opened his hand to show her the coloured stones the magpie had brought. "They're tesserae. Roman mosaic tiles. I think there's a Roman temple full of treasure under that wood. All we need to do is call the British Museum and they'll come and protect the wood."

Orla gasped and held out a hand. "Tom..."

"No," he sniffed. "I've been trying to tell you for days and you always tell me to shut up."

He was really upset now – the fear and distress of this so-called holiday gushing out on a river of hot tears.

"Tom, I'm sorry," said Orla. "I really am sorry for ignoring you, but there's no temple under Anna's Wood. It's much worse than that."

Tom glared at her, his lip trembling, wet streaks on his red cheeks. "Just forget it," he yelled, then turned and ran.

Richard arrived back an hour later, politely knocking on the door of the smokehouse as Orla was preparing her potions, still feeling guilty.

"It's safe," called Orla as Richard poked his nose fearfully into the candlelit room.

"Where's Raven?" he asked.

"With Dave," said Orla.

"So where's Dave?"

"Er…" mumbled Orla, grinding horehound in a mortar. "I might have seen her in the back of a police car heading east."

"Oh my God!"

"She'll be fine," reasoned Orla. "She's got Dave with her." She turned to look at her brother. "And they're both safer there than we are here. How did it go with the posters?"

"All gone," he said. "I've come back to print more."

"The more the better," nodded Orla. "Tom's really upset, by the way. He thinks there's a Roman temple full of treasure under the wood."

"If only it was that simple," muttered Richard. He watched Orla as she dripped dragon's blood into a green bottle. His attention was immensely distracting.

"What?" she said. The air smelled of plant sap, spirit and anxiety.

"Look at us," said Richard. "Hiding out on a marsh, me printing propaganda posters, you making... What exactly are you making?"

"Magic potions," said Orla.

"Magic potions," muttered Richard, shaking his head. "We're resistance fighters struggling against an evil army that would kill us if they found us. Do you want to live this way?"

Orla looked at him. The pungent odour of the concoction was making her eyes water. "Not really," she sniffed.

Richard nodded. "Me neither." He turned to leave the smokehouse, pausing in the doorway. "But I think this is our fate. Did the magpie show you that?"

By 6 p.m., Orla was ready: potion prepared, lines practised and mind clear. Except for two little shadows. She dabbed Malasana with oil of the moon and tied a necklace of dried rowan berries around the doll's neck, whispering, "Rowan berries from the holy tree, push all evil away from me." Then she packed the potions, her penknife, a pair of wire cutters and five jam jars into her backpack and headed back over the footbridge to the house.

Tom was in the kitchen, nailing heavy timber to the broken back door. He'd fixed a board over the broken window too.

"Nice work," said Orla.

"It might help," he mumbled. "The kettle's on." He seemed to be in a slightly better mood.

"Any sign of the others?" Orla pulled back a scorched curtain and peered across the marsh.

"Richard's upstairs washing his hair; Raven and Dave are still missing in action. Quiet, isn't it?"

Orla nodded. "Too quiet."

"Do you think Godric Thorn has given up?"

"I wish," she said, biting into a soft apple. "He's not the sort to give up."

The kettle whistled. Outside, a flight of greylag geese honked as they passed overhead, and from far away came the startled quacking of disturbed ducks. Tom poured herbs into a brown teapot, then added water and stirred.

"Will the next attack be worse?" he asked softly, his voice trembling.

Orla looked at him as she chewed her apple. She nodded. "Probably."

Tom kept stirring. "OK," he said quietly. He wasn't, though.

As Orla stood up to give him a hug, the back door burst open. Dave sprinted in, black with liquid mud. He jumped up to greet Orla and Tom, splattering them, then leapt onto the sofa and off again – leaving filthy paw prints on the cushions – and up onto the kitchen table where he growled at Vinegar Tom and stood dead centre, wagging his tail in triumph. Behind him was Raven, equally muddy and stumbling because she was laughing so hard.

Orla looked at them both. "And?"

Raven flopped on the sofa and grinned. "We're fugitives from the law."

"What happened?" Orla suddenly felt like the parent in the room.

"Oh my God," gushed Raven. "It was so cool. We broke into the GasFrac compound and cut the hydraulic lines on five diggers—"

"Bulldozers," interrupted Tom. "Caterpillar D10T2s."

Raven shrugged. "Whatever. Then this massive German shepherd came after us, but Dave fought him off. Have you seen him when he's angry? He's mental."

That explained why Dave was so pleased with himself, thought Orla.

"We ran away, and as we were coming across the marsh,

GasFrac put up a drone to chase us. Then the police turned up. We could have shaken them off easily but it was better to let them catch us there instead of leading them here. So we surrendered."

"How did the warrior feel about that?" asked Orla, nodding at her exceedingly smug, horribly dirty dog.

"Initially unconvinced, I'd say," said Raven. "Anyway, it gets better. They put us in the back of a police car and said they were taking us to Norwich police station. I started telling them exactly what GasFrac were up to and I think one of them was actually quite interested, but Dave had launched a chemical attack with those really pungent farts and we saw the burned-out post office and all these villagers queuing at the doctor's surgery. They all had dog bites, and when they saw Dave in the police car there was mass panic. It was really weird.

"Then we had to make a detour to some place called Burnham Out or something because there was a disturbance."

"Burnham Down," said Orla, allowing Raven to take a breath.

"Yeah, and there was this big woman in a flowery dress chasing dogs around the village shouting 'Give it back!' and when she saw Dave she went, like, really, really, really crazy…"

Orla looked at Dave. He snapped half-heartedly at his wasp and returned the look of big-eyed innocence that was a clear sign of his participation in some deeply disturbing yet plausibly deniable black ops shenanigans.

"She was yelling 'He's got it; he's got it!' and telling the cops to arrest Dave; and when they said they already had, she said they should arrest him again and while the policemen were trying to calm her down, we sort of slipped away."

Raven finally came to a stop and gave a big cheesy grin that somehow lifted Orla's heart. "So here we are. What's for dinner?"

Orla shrugged. "Dunno. What's for dinner, Tom?"

Tom looked in the fridge. "Beetroot," he said. "With celery and ketchup."

CHAPTER 25

Dinner was grim, and as Raven miserably scraped the ketchup from her plate with a stick of limp celery, Orla stood up.

"I'll be going out at ten thirty," she announced. "I should be back by half past two. I've repaired and recharged all the protective charms with sprowl from Vinegar Tom and added extras at the weak points from last night." She pointed at the kitchen window. "One of you needs to be keeping watch from here at all times. They can only approach from that direction. There's a new pentagram – bigger and more powerful than last night – on Uncle Valentine's bedroom floor. If they come, you know the drill."

A fearful silence fell over Sicow's Creek as each considered how this night might end.

Then Richard cleared his throat. "In a rare piece of good news, I have an announcement to make. My other holiday project is complete. We can watch TV tonight."

As Tom kept first watch the others crammed onto

the damp sofa to watch the local news. A reporter was standing outside the post office in Haddenham St Taylan – still sealed off with police crime scene tape – explaining how the postmistress, a respected local figure, had yet to be found.

It was not yet known if the fire was connected with what psychiatrists were calling "a rare example of mass hysteria" there and in the neighbouring village of Burnham Down. Several members of the community had turned up at their local surgeries with dog bites and scratches they were at a loss to explain. "Some wags – excuse the pun – have suggested a werewolf is responsible," joked the journalist.

Dave, sat at the kids' feet, wagged his tail. Werewolf One wasn't a bad call sign.

"Haddenham St Taylan," continued the reporter, "is, of course, the nearest village to the Anna's Wood gas extraction site, four miles to the west, where clearance operations are scheduled to begin at seven o'clock on Monday morning. No representative from the energy company was available for interview this evening, but in a statement GasFrac said it wanted to reassure residents that disruption will be kept to a minimum as the ninety-acre woodland is cut down.

"It is not thought," concluded the journalist, "that the post office fire is connected with the gas fracking operation."

Orla leaned in for a closer look, and the picture disintegrated into a fuzz of electric bees. So much for Richard's repair. She stood up and walked away, and as she did so, the picture returned. The news was over and a weather reporter was saying that a deep trough of low pressure was bringing strong winds and long periods of heavy rain, perhaps leading to local flooding, along the North Norfolk coast.

"Brilliant," muttered Orla, putting on her yellow sou'wester. "Right, I'm going to Anna's Wood to do some witchcraft. Remember the drills." She snapped Dave into his tactical harness, lowered the moth-eaten stuffed cat into a carrier bag and then covered it with another.

"Can I come?" asked Raven.

Orla wished she could. "No. The book of spells makes it clear that a Traumnebel must be performed in utter solitude because we are all alone in our dreams."

"Wow," said Raven. "That's deep."

"So how come Dave gets to go?" asked Tom.

"Because he's my familiar," explained Orla.

Close protection specialist, actually, thought Dave, wriggling his harness into place.

Some singer Orla had never heard of was receiving rapturous applause on *The Graham Norton Show*. She slipped on her backpack and hesitated by the back door.

"Bye, then."

Raven dashed across and grabbed Orla's arms. "I can't let you do this alone."

"We should come at least part of the way," agreed Richard, standing up.

"We can wait for you at the bridge," suggested Raven.

"We can guard your bike," added Tom.

Orla smiled. Having her bike stolen was the least of her concerns. "And who's going to look after Uncle Valentine? I'll be fine." She lifted Dave. "I've got the dog, remember?"

That deep trough of low pressure had yet to arrive at Sicow's Creek but the winds were already scouring the marsh, beating down the marram grass with explosive gusts and threatening to blow Orla, Dave, Vinegar Tom and the bike into the creek. Progress was slow – not just because of the gale but because she dared not turn on her headlamp. You never knew who was watching and, despite the weather, it was still too quiet.

All three versions in Miss Lamorna Teague's red book of spells had made it clear that the Traumnebel had to be performed on the sinister side of a compass under a waxing moon. Orla could draw the compass, but she could do nothing about the moon. Up there, behind the clouds, was a waning crescent: a moon made for mischief and malfeasance; but since she had no choice in the matter, it was a risk she would have to take. She took a deep breath and pedalled faster, feeling the sickly radiation from Vinegar Tom and the disgust of a Jack Russell forced to share a bicycle basket with a cat, albeit a dead one.

It took sixteen minutes to reach the bridge over the Swallow, cycling beneath trees that swished like wet mops over a road shiny with the first heavy drops of rain. Hiding her bike behind a blackthorn, Orla checked her watch: 10.59 p.m.

"Let's go, dog," she whispered, lifting Vinegar Tom from the bike basket, but Dave didn't move. He stood under a bush, one paw lifted, staring down the lane.

"Come on," urged Orla, but Dave was going to stay put until he was absolutely certain they hadn't been followed. It took him six long minutes to reach that conclusion, after which he trotted past Orla and along the slippery path up the valley towards the wood.

There were no bird calls tonight – the barn owls were too clever to go outside when the rain would soak their feathers – and the only sounds were the rustling of hedgehogs, the distant bark of a vixen and the wind in the trees, its sighs turning to groans that would soon become howls.

"Keep watch," ordered Orla. Staying low in the long, wet grass, she crept along the fence line to the river, but

GasFrac had closed that gap in their defences with a double wall dug into the river bed.

"Drat," murmured Orla. She slid the wire cutters from her pack and began snipping the chain links. Suddenly Dave was alongside her, her cuff in his teeth as he tried to pull her hand away. "Get off," she hissed, shaking her hand free, but he came back, growling and tugging until Orla saw the thin red alarm wire lying in the jaws of her wire cutters.

"Oops," she said. "Well done, dog. That could have been awkward."

It took ten minutes to cut the hole, after which Dave darted through, nose close to the ground as he checked for tripwires and other sensors. Orla followed, feeling now more than ever the oppressive nothingness of Anna's Wood. The heart of the void was in the middle of the sighing wood, right on the riverbank, so it would be there that she performed the ritual. She dropped to her knees and yelped as bone hit rock. Delving into the wet leaf litter, her fingers scratched across a boulder.

Not a boulder. A square-edged block of granite.

"Handy," muttered Orla, brushing away the leaves, shrugging off her backpack and setting up on the slab the tools of her craft: the potions, matches, a knife, the hare's skull she'd brought from home, a stripped stick of blackthorn, a tot of Uncle Valentine's rum, the ball of red wool, a dead cat and five jam jars she'd taken from the workshop. She checked her watch: 11.48 p.m. The book of spells stated that the best times for a dream cast were seven minutes to midnight and four minutes past four. That left just five minutes, but despite her beating heart, dry mouth and hollow stomach, Orla was ready.

She'd succeeded in casting spells against the odds in the past and she could do it again if only she let her subconscious, that part of her mind that drew wisdom from her DNA, rule her hand and heart. And that wasn't going to happen with Dave running around like an anxious teacher on a school outing.

"Dog," she whispered. "Skedaddle."

Dave padded away to keep watch from the high ground, and Orla stood up, stretched and began the rite of purification. Tonight, by the grace of Bucca Dhu, the Lord of Flint, the people of Norfolk would see the truth and the law of nature would prevail. Three magpies, woken by the two intruders, flitted silently into an oak tree where once a Larsen trap had hung to watch the show. One dropped something, but Orla was too focused on performing the ritual to notice.

A Traumnebel is a long and extraordinarily complicated process involving a compass circle, a stick and a flame; and

265

spirit and magic potions that must contain exactly the right ratios of ingredients. You also need enough sprowl to light up a city. The basic principle is to take the message from your mind, place it into the skull of a hare and then call upon the spirit of the south road – the white hare – to deliver that message like a rolling bank of fog to all whose minds are open. Since human minds are at their most accessible in the absence of consciousness, the spell is best performed while the audience is asleep. But it's a conjuring where almost anything can go wrong. Since your message, taken from your mind, is no more than a thought, it can be drowned out by external interference: a church bell chiming; an aircraft passing overhead; a dog barking because he can sense a witch – even the ticking of a watch or the hooting of a roosting owl.

But Orla persisted, her words and actions driven by invisible genetic memories, not daring to consider for a moment if she was getting it right, because if the trance was broken, the Traumnebel would end as though the plug had been pulled on a TV.

She almost made it.

Then Dave started barking.

"Orla Perry," seethed Godric Thorn.

CHAPTER 26

He was standing halfway up the west bank in a long black coat, leaning on a furled umbrella and watching as Dave ran snarling at him, his teeth sharp and gleaming. As he pounced, Godric flicked his fingers and Dave dropped, gasping for breath as invisible coils wrapped around his throat.

"Leave him alone!" cried Orla.

"If I can conjure an imaginary wasp, I can conjure a serpent," sighed Godric. "But it won't kill him; I can't take the pain. But you, Orla Perry, you deserve death. Do you know how many workers I lost last night, apart from the lovely Kevin?"

He snapped his fingers and Orla's legs collapsed. She fell in the centre of her compass, fighting to keep her trance state like someone rudely awakened trying to hold on to a dream. She could see magpies at the edge of her vision. Were they carrying the Traumnebel's message?

"Witchcraft is an exhausting business, isn't it?" said Godric. "Anyway, the answer is one hundred and nine.

One hundred and nine of the world's finest minds burned out last night. All gone, and all because a stubborn, inconsequential little witch wants to take me on. It's quite unbelievable."

The birds were launching themselves from their roosts: the blackbirds, jays, woodpeckers, redstarts and magpies Orla had promised to save. Maybe they weren't helping her spread the truth to the people. Maybe they knew their home was lost and were simply leaving. Godric glanced up at them, then popped his umbrella as though expecting an attack.

He was so angry that he was walking in little circles, first clockwise, then anticlockwise under his twirling umbrella. Orla was trying to keep the connection open with the white hare but the vision was fading fast.

"When the replacements arrive I'll get some of them to devise a series of unfortunate accidents to befall your family and friends. Once it starts, it will not stop, and you should know that you will be the last to die."

From somewhere behind him, Dave was wrestling his invisible snake. Godric stormed down the slope, almost stepping into the hallowed circle.

"I've won, Orla Perry, and you've lost. You've all lost, but while the villagers think Anna's Wood is just about gas and trees, you and I know the truth. This is the northern junction of the ancient roads of life and death: the Ana and Patallo ley lines. The Romans knew how powerful it was, so they built a temple dedicated to Diana right here. No expense was spared. Mosaics from Ephesus, priests from Patara, gold and jewels from the outer edges of the empire; and then, as Rome fell apart, they abandoned it. A century after they left, no trace of the complex remained. The pagans dismantled it and buried it."

He pointed at the high ground with its swaying, dripping beeches. "Under there lies hidden one of the seven most hallowed sites in the northern hemisphere. If the Christians had known, they'd have built a cathedral here and this wood would have become a huge city – an English Rome or Jerusalem. Amazing, isn't it?"

Orla felt the strength draining from her arms and neck. She was emerging from the trance, losing the hare. And then, with a sigh, and the damp flutter of the last departing magpie, it was gone. She lay on her back. Vinegar Tom fell over and, one by one, the candles in the jam jars went out. Her mind flickered with the fragment of a memory from the night the one-footed magpie had shown her the future. She'd interpreted the high stone walls, the terraces and the naked flames as parts of a gas extraction plant. Now she realized that what she'd seen was a temple. Tom was right.

"You don't need this place," she said softly. "You've got dozens of sites already."

"Thirteen, actually," said Godric. "There are only thirteen."

Orla sat up. "One less won't hurt."

"But it will," he protested. "I need to control all thirteen points of the Treskaidekastron."

He pushed his hands into his pockets and tapped a rock with the toe of his shoe. "I told you already, Orla Perry: there are two types of people in my world. Employees and enemies. Sometimes one can be both, of course. The fate of all is in my hands, and look…" He bent and picked up a jam jar, squeezing it between thumb and forefinger until it shattered.

"Lives are so easily crushed, but a girl like you is still more useful alive than dead." He licked his hand and smiled bashfully, his lips streaked with blood. "In seventeen centuries I have never given anyone a second chance, but look at me now, standing in the rain and breaking the habit of many lifetimes." He shrugged. "I must be getting soft.

"Here's the thing. Option one: work for me. Option two: watch your friends and family get taken away by one inexplicably freakish calamity after another. You've seen how quickly the weather changed for your uncle." He snapped his fingers, and somewhere in the dark Dave yelped. "I'm giving you until the first tree in this wood falls to make up your mind."

He twirled his umbrella and ascended the bank, turning as he reached the top and slapping an oak. "Let's call this one the Orla Perry Tree of Life." Using the silver tip of his umbrella, he scratched OPTL in the bark. It cut like a laser, leaving the odour of scorched wood hanging in the night.

"I'll tell my men to cut this tree first, and when it falls, my offer expires." He rooted in the dead leaves with the tip of a shoe, then bent to pick something up.

"Check this out," he said, flipping something glittery through the air. It dropped at Orla's feet: a thumbnail-sized golden amulet engraved with the head of a bird. "There's treasure everywhere you look in this wood."

He raised his eyebrows and held a bloody thumb and forefinger to his ear like a phone. "Call me."

CHAPTER 27

Slowly Orla gathered up her tools, her jars, the dead cat and the golden amulet and packed them carefully away. She was concentrating on the task in a vain effort to keep her disappointment and fear at bay. Dave lay beside her, his cheek in the mud, his body bruised and exhausted.

"I've messed up again, dog," she whispered. "Big time."

His ears twitched and he raised his head.

"It's OK," she soothed. "Stand down." She glanced up at the Orla Perry Tree of Life. "I can't stop Monday coming."

Accepting Godric's offer promised riches, power and certain death. The alternative was ... certain death. Faces flashed through her mind: Dad, Mum, Richard, Tom, Raven, Uncle Valentine and Dave. None of them would be safe unless she signed up to the forces of evil. She had just two days to decide.

"Drat," she yelled, hurling her backpack across the clearing. "Drat, drat, drat, drat, drat." She snatched it up, swung it over her shoulders, stuffed Vinegar Tom under her arm and started walking. "Let's go."

Too depressed and ashamed to return to Sicow's Creek, she followed the dyke across the marsh to the beach she'd never seen. She'd known at their first meeting that she was no match for Godric Thorn, but her pride had ignored the warnings and now the lives of everyone she loved were at stake. She'd been stupid, arrogant and selfish and now the only way to save her friends and family was to literally surrender her soul.

Oblivious to the driving rain and thumping wind, she stumbled over a wall of dunes onto the beach. The North Sea was another half-mile away, the roar of the surf like a distant round of applause: the cruel ocean applauding the antics of a clown with dripping corkscrew hair and her faithful, limping dog.

Something darker than the night loomed ahead: the upturned hull of Uncle Valentine's boat half buried in the sands and backlit by the arc lights in the GasFrac compound a mile to the west. She sat on the wet sand in the lee of the boat. Dave hopped painfully onto the timbers to keep watch, and Orla smiled sadly. Her dog was never off duty and yet all his loyalty and protection counted for nothing now. She patted the sand, inviting him to sit beside her, but he didn't come. She tilted her head back to call him, but he wasn't listening. His hackles were up, his ears were cocked and a low growl was rattling in his throat, shivering through the timbers and into the hard sand.

Except it wasn't Dave who was making the ground shake.

Orla stood up. Orange lights were flashing in the GasFrac compound and the wind carried the roar and smell of revving diesel engines. She checked her watch: 2.39 a.m. The bulldozers were on the move – more than forty-eight hours earlier than expected. Godric had changed the timings to launch a surprise attack and she had until the first tree fell before the accidents started happening.

She grabbed Vinegar Tom and started running, back across the beach, over the dunes and onto the dyke path, Dave leading the way. Time was running out. She had to call Godric right now.

She met Raven, Richard and Tom coming across the footbridge.

"GasFrac are on the move," cried Raven. "They're not supposed to begin until Monday. I've left a voice message for the chief planning officer." Her commando beanie was crowned with a green headlamp and her face was daubed in black.

Dave wagged his tail. He liked her style.

"Tell me the Traumnebel worked," she begged, gripping

274

Orla's arm. She peered into her friend's eyes and frowned when she saw the truth. "That's a no, isn't it? Oh, Orla. I'm so sorry."

"Godric arrived at the crucial moment and broke it," she confessed. "I don't know how, but he knew I'd be there. I failed." She shook her arm free. "Someone give me a phone. I need to call him."

"He's hardly going to reconsider now, is he?" said Richard. He was wearing a dark blue turtleneck and his face too was smeared in black.

The guttural roar of tank-sized diesel engines arrived on the wind.

"They'll transport them on low-loaders," said Tom. "Stops the tracks mashing up the roads." With his hoody and bandana, he looked like a street protester.

"He will listen," insisted Orla. "He's expecting my call."

"What do you mean?" asked Raven, confused.

Orla looked at her. At Richard. At Tom. "I'm going to make a deal with him."

"What kind of deal?" asked Richard suspiciously.

"I'm going to work for him."

There was a moment of shocked silence.

Then Tom said, "You what?"

"He's offered me a deal. If I join Thorn Corp, you'll all stay safe."

"You don't make deals with Godric Thorn," argued Raven. "He can kill us all any time he likes, whatever he says."

"You know that's not true," said Orla. "He's evil, but he can't lie. None of us can." She lowered her gaze. "Us witches, I mean. And I've made my choice."

"You're choosing death," said Tom. "You heard what Kevin said. You don't retire from Thorn Corp. You expire."

Orla shrugged. "We can work that out later. Just give me a phone."

Richard stuffed his hands in his pockets, as though worried Orla might levitate his phone. "Why the rush?"

"Because he's waiting."

Raven scoffed. "Let the creep wait."

"And in the meantime," said Richard, "we can try and stop that convoy."

"You're crazy!" exclaimed Orla. Now she'd stopped running, she was feeling the cold. "What can four kids and a dog do against a convoy of bulldozers?"

"You could do a spell," suggested Tom.

"No, I can't," said Orla. "There's no more sprowl except what little lies in these." She rummaged in her pocket and pulled out the tiles the magpie had brought. "You were right, Tom. I should have listened to you. These really are

Roman tesserae and you were the only one who got the message. There is a temple in the wood. Pagans buried it and planted trees on top of it. Godric told me."

Raven started as though electrocuted. "A Roman temple?" she gasped.

"A massive temple of Diana," said Orla. "The pagans tore it down and buried it in the sixth century to stop the Christians building a cathedral on their site." She stuffed a hand in her jeans pocket and pulled out the golden amulet. "This was just lying on the surface. Godric found it and gave it to me."

"Oh my God." Raven grinned. "This changes everything." Her hand flew to her pocket, and with shaking fingers she pulled out her phone. "You don't need to call Godric Thorn; you need to call Neville Clearly, the chief planning officer. We can stop this now. Let's find a signal."

She sprinted up the track. Richard raised his eyebrows and put his arm around Orla. "We'll be fine," he said. "You wait and see. But there's just one little thing. Can I see that piece of Roman gold again?"

As Orla held out the amulet, Richard snatched it and flicked it into the creek. "That's better," he said. "Didn't Mum tell you never to accept anything from strangers?"

When they caught up with Raven, she was holding her phone in the air in a desperate bid to find a single bar of signal. "I was right here twenty minutes ago," she fumed. "It was working then."

Richard was checking his own phone. "No service," he confirmed. "Do you think Godric has killed the tower?"

"Damn, damn, damn, damn," seethed Raven. "We're on our own."

Flashing lights, all Halloween orange, were in the lane behind the trees. Yellow headlight beams pierced the rain. The faint crackle of radios drifted over the grinding of gears.

"They're on the move," said Richard. "If we can't stop them, we can at least slow them down." He handed Orla a pair of yellow bolt cutters: a heavy, two-handed tool with wickedly sharp teeth. "These are for you."

"To cut the brake pipes," added Tom.

"And lose the yellow raincoat," ordered Raven. "You look like a canary."

CHAPTER 28

The convoy was moving along the lane at walking place: a belching line of twenty-wheel low-loaders carrying mustard yellow seventy-tonne bulldozers gleaming in the flashing lights.

"If we can stop the first one, we stop the whole convoy," said Raven.

"And if we can stop the last one, they'll be trapped," added Richard.

"You've thought about this, haven't you?" observed Orla.

"Graham Norton was boring," said Richard. "Now you've turned up we can operate in pairs. Orla and Tom, take the lead; Raven and I will take the rear."

"No," argued Raven. "Orla and I work better together. You go with Tom."

"Girls versus boys." Tom shrugged. "What does Dave do?"

Dave knew his role in this op. Force protection,

providing security to the sabotage teams. He gave a soft woof in confirmation.

"The brake hoses are behind the cab of each truck, so we need to climb aboard, cut them and skedaddle," said Raven. She pointed east to where the road descended to the three-arch bridge over the Swallow River. "If we get it right, the first truck will lose control on that slope. The others won't be able to pass because of the river, and they won't be able to back out because the last truck in line will also be out of action." She looked at Orla. "Clever, right?"

"That's genius," replied Orla. Her jumper was soaking up the rain and sucking the heat from her body.

"Show of arms," ordered Richard.

"Chopper," said Tom, wielding a gleaming hatchet.

"Brake hose snips," confirmed Raven.

"Bolt cutters," said Orla.

"And I've got the axe," said Richard. He looked at the carrier bag in Orla's hand. "You need to lose the dead cat. You'll want both hands free."

"Fine," said Orla, shrugging off her backpack. "I'll stuff him in here."

"It's going to get very nasty, very quickly, out there," said Richard gravely. "We need to avoid capture at all costs, get the job done and regroup at the wood."

"Left bank of the Swallow, where the fence meets the water, I've cut a hole," said Orla.

Raven nodded. "Nice. Let's be careful out there."

The first truck was a hundred yards away, lights flashing like a Transformer, rain glittering on its windscreen like diamonds and the face of its driver glowing faintly in the dashboard light. Orla and Raven lay flat in the wet grass, feeling the ground trembling as the behemoth approached. Suddenly it was alongside: a smoking dinosaur of rubber and steel bearing a monstrous yellow bulldozer on its back.

Raven gripped Orla's arm. "Now," she hissed, leaping to her feet and gripping the ladder behind the cab. By the time Orla was on her feet, Raven was already on the beast's back, her hand extended to pull Orla up. The deck was slippery in the rain, the pipes greasy.

"Which hose?" asked Orla.

"I dunno." Raven shrugged, her face strobing under the flashing orange lights. "All of them?" She pushed her brake hose cutting snips against the nearest.

Hooking an arm behind a hose to steady herself, Orla opened the jaws of her bolt cutters. There was an explosive hiss, a nasty thump and half a scream as a severed pipe writhed like a cut snake. When Orla looked up, Raven was gone. She stepped across the footplate and glanced back along the lane to see Dave darting to a dark patch in the ditch. Was that Raven? Her heart pounded. There wasn't time to check. She cut the pipes high, and then ducked.

From behind her, an air horn blared long and loud. She'd been spotted. The truck lurched to a stop and she heard the crackle of the radio as the driver's door was thrown open. A man appeared on the ladder, rain dripping from his yellow helmet, his mouth gaping in shock. Orla dropped to the platform as he mounted the ladder, seizing the nearest hose in the jaws of her bolt cutters.

"What the bl—" yelled the driver as Orla cut the pipe. It lashed across the plate like a crocodile's tail, thumping into his chest and hurling him from the truck. Orla reached up to cut the last five, but there was no time. Torch beams were piercing the night air; radios were blaring.

Trouble was coming. Avoid capture at all costs.

Orla jumped from the platform.

"Oi!" yelled a voice from the dark. "Stop right there!"

She climbed the ladder into the cab, slammed the door and thumped the lock. How on earth did this thing work? There was a steering wheel, two foot pedals, a lever with a P on it, a red light with *brake pressure* written on it that was flashing urgently, and an angry man with a beard and a construction helmet banging even more urgently on the window. Orla stamped on the big pedal. Nothing happened. She tried the other and the truck roared. She pressed a button and the cab filled with the sound of Bonnie Tyler singing "Holding Out for a Hero". The man yelled again, shaking his arm – which now had a Jack Russell attached to it.

Orla pulled the lever and stamped on the small pedal; the truck lurched forward and the man disappeared. She rolled twenty yards, then pressed the big pedal. The truck kept rolling so, holding the wheel with one hand, she opened the driver's door. Dave was jogging alongside, far below.

"Get in," she called and Dave leapt, scrabbling on the ladder and dropping away. "Come on, dog," urged Orla as he failed a second time. "You can do it."

And he could, getting high enough on the third attempt for Orla to grab his tactical harness and drag him into the cab. Orla pressed the accelerator, feeling the awesome power of the six hundred horsepower diesel engine. The road began to dip, and there, in the headlights, was the three-arch bridge.

Orla glanced at Dave and grinned. "Let's get some air."

Dave winced. The truck's brake hoses had been cut and it was speeding downhill towards a narrow bridge. This was going to be messy. He checked Orla, her hair all over her mud-splatted face, her hands stained with grease and oil, her green eyes glowing with a manic inner fire. Then he glanced through the rear window to the monstrous bulldozer on the trailer. Running an urgent risk assessment, Dave concluded that when they hit the bridge, seventy tonnes of steel would slide forward and crush the cab like a tin can. He gave a loud warning bark and looked at the door.

"What?" called Orla.

He barked again.

"Oh." Orla nodded. "You think we should vacate the vehicle?"

Dave danced on the seat, barking and wagging his tail. She got it.

Orla reached across, scooped him into her arms and kicked open the driver's door. It was a long way down to fast-moving tarmac. She looked up. Colliding with the bridge would hurt more, so she jumped, hitting the road with bended knees and rolling into a blackthorn bush as the screech and roar of steel smashing into stone, the hiss of steam and the manic tinkle of breaking glass filled the night.

Orla rubbed her elbow and looked at Dave. Dave raised his eyebrows.

"We're in so much trouble," she said.

Boots were thumping on the road. Torch beams wobbled through the air. Walkie-talkies squawked. Then Richard and Tom appeared, sprinting towards the wreckage.

"Detain those idiots," barked a voice.

Orla pushed forward, peeking through the blackthorn to see Godric Thorn in a black coat and a halo of orange light standing on the brow of the hill as security guards ran past. He looked directly at her, as though he could see through darkness and chaos. Then he signalled to a big bald-headed man.

"Unload the bulldozers," he commanded, pointing at Anna's Wood. "We'll go across the fields."

He raised a radio to his lips. "Bring those two brats to my vehicle; there's a Lamborghini for the man who captures the girl. Repeat: a Lamborghini."

Orla glanced back towards the wreckage. GasFrac security guards Trev and Lee, who had twice failed to trap Orla, were marching Richard up the lane, Ace limping alongside, his leg bandaged after that afternoon's meeting with Dave. Richard was arguing with his captors, struggling to break free, but they were too strong. There was no sign of Tom, and Raven was gone.

Orla looked at Dave. It was just the two of them now.

CHAPTER 29

The plan was to regroup at the wood. Dave led the way, swimming beside Orla as she waded downstream of the bridge, crossing the road on the far side and moving fast and low up the valley. To the east, towards the turn-off for St Taylan's Hill, blue lights were flashing.

The creaking of steel and roar of powerful diesel engines ripped through the night as icy white headlight beams flashed through the rain. Orla glanced across the river and back towards the lane. Those flashing blue lights were approaching from the east as the bulldozers were being driven off their trailers. One had already ripped through the hedge and into the field, its tracks creaking as they churned through the shivering barley. Chainsaw-wielding men in helmets followed it, like infantrymen advancing behind a tank.

Orla ran on, her boots slipping on the muddy riverbank. The brief pause had allowed the adrenaline to subside, and now she felt cold, sick and so worried about Raven and her brothers that her legs were turning to jelly. The battle seemed lost. The first bulldozer would be here within the next five minutes, and even if she could stop that one, the others would find a way past her and into the wood. But she couldn't give up. Dave wouldn't let her.

She reached the steel fence, jumped into the river and waded to the west bank. Following the fence line she came to the edge of the barley field where once, so long ago, it seemed, she had emerged after rescuing a magpie. It was as good a place as any to make a last stand.

She stuffed Malasana and the distress flares she'd taken from the rope-house inside her jacket, then leaned backwards, pressing her backpack against the fence and reaching behind her to grip the wire in her fingers. Dave took up position slightly in front of her and to her left, protecting the flank.

Five yellow monsters were roaring across the field now, rain in their headlights, black smoke and mud in their wake.

She knew she wouldn't die here because Godric was saving her for last. Dave, on the other hand, had until the men with the chainsaws pushed past her, found the Orla Perry Tree of Life and hacked it down. Once it fell, the accidents would start.

The Battle of Anna's Wood was under way and she was hopelessly outnumbered.

Suddenly the first bulldozer was just twenty-five yards away, its tracks churning a spray of mud and its serrated blade at neck height. Twenty-five yards became fifteen, then five, and as Orla took a deep breath it ground to a lurching halt, its engine coughing and that wicked blade only an arm's length away. The driver raised a walkie-talkie, slowly and carefully, like a man reporting an unexpected encounter with a tiger that could pounce at any moment.

"This is driver number nine claiming the Lamborghini," he said, very quietly. "The girl is at the security fence." The four men riding the flanks jumped down, their chainsaws at the ready and the beams from their headlamps poking spookily through the murk.

"Get her, then," urged driver number nine.

"You get her," retorted one of the men.

"I'm driving the bulldozer," insisted driver number nine.

Dave was still barking, his tone half a notch above *I'll rip your face off.*

"That's all you'll be driving if you don't deliver her to the boss," noted another.

Driver number nine sighed. "Oi, kid," he called to Orla. "Come here."

"Come and get me," shouted Orla.

The driver stood up as two more bulldozers arrived.

"You can't win, you know. You can stand in front of me all night but you can't stop them." He waved to the other drivers, pointing west. "Take the fence down over there and find the boss's special tree, lads," he said into his radio. "I'm being held up by a mad kid with a doll."

One of the saw men had been edging closer to Orla and chose now to make a lunge. A bad idea, he quickly realized, as a furious Jack Russell attacked him in a blur of tooth and claw. Another tried to grab Orla's arm, but Dave whirled back, leaping for his throat and putting him to flight. As two more charged, Orla fired her first flare. The projectile rocketed over their heads and exploded halfway across the field. To the left, workmen had reached the fence and were using spanners to loosen the bolts securing the panels. Orla took a deep breath then sprinted towards them, firing her second flare and screaming like a banshee.

Suddenly she wasn't alone. The chattering of magpies filled the night like the cackling of witches as a vast flock arrived from the east, diving on the workmen, pecking with beaks, scratching with talons and guaranteeing all a glimpse of their future. Spanners fell into wet grass as men covered their faces and fled for shelter, but now there was an attack from the right flank. Dave broke off the pursuit of a saw man to rush back to the riverbank, where a new force was crossing the Swallow – led by a short man in a tweed suit and, behind him, what looked like an ageing emperor in a chair borne on the shoulders of strong men.

"Mr Flaherty?" gasped Orla.

He smiled at her. "No one moves heavy plant in these parts without my knowing about it. I sent some of the lads to Sicow's Creek to fetch your uncle. He deserves to see this showdown." He glanced up at the chair. "Doesn't he look regal carried aloft on his throne?"

The emperor raised a hand and the column halted. His throne was a rickety dining chair.

"That chair belongs in the kitchen," scolded Orla. "And you should be at home, in bed."

"So should you," retorted Uncle Valentine. "And I thought I told you to stay away from this wood." He waved a hand at the muddy field, the yellow bulldozers with their flashing lights and the crowd wading across the river to stop them. "Now look what you've done."

"It's your fault," she countered. "You said it was worth a try." She reached up and touched his hand. "And you were right."

"It's not saved yet, girl," said Mr Flaherty. He turned to his men. "Patrick and Michael, take the lads and see if you can get the keys from those Caterpillars."

Dozens – perhaps hundreds – were still crossing the river. Orla saw Charlie Cement Wings and Crepuscular

Ray among a citizen army of men and women, the oldest in her nineties, the youngest a baby in a carrier on her mother's back. Many wore bandages on their hands or had scratch marks on their faces, as though they'd lost a fight with a dog. She heard shouts of "Shame on you, GasFrac!" and snatches of excited conversation.

"I really believe in the power of dreams," gushed a man wearing running tights and a Guy Fawkes mask. "It was so wonderfully vivid."

"I know." A woman in a pink hoody nodded. "And did you hear the noise those birds were making?"

"More like one of them visions than a dream," confirmed another, armed with a golf club. "Did you hear they arrested Jemima Water-Mills?"

The villagers pushed past Orla, forming a line between the bulldozers and the wood. Then Orla felt eyes on her.

Godric Thorn was standing beside driver number nine's bulldozer, twirling his umbrella like an irritated cat flicking its tail. Trev, Lee and Ace stood behind him, looking as though they were seriously considering a change of career.

"I've never had children," called Godric, looking straight at Orla, "but I believe this is what happens when they're not properly supervised."

The big men from the traveller site were closing in on him fast.

"Gentlemen," he called. "Will you let me try and explain myself?"

Mr Flaherty raised a hand. His men stopped.

"Keep it brief, Mr Thorn," called Uncle Valentine. He looked like Zeus from where Orla was standing.

The magpies whirled into the trees as the crowd began chanting, "Shame on you, shame on you, shame on you."

Godric closed his eyes, dropped his umbrella and lowered his head, letting the rain run down his face like tears. He let the mob have the floor for exactly one minute, then raised his hands.

"Citizens," he called out, "I beg you: there is no need for this." He paused, and the chanting died away. "I accept completely that the planning order says we cannot begin clearing the wood until Monday but by moving at the weekend while the roads were empty, I thought I would be helping to avoid causing congestion at the start of the working week."

He bent to lift a discarded chainsaw, carefully brushed the mud from its blade and placed it in the cab of the bulldozer. "I realize that in doing so," he continued, "I have made a mistake. Betrayed your trust, and I apologize profoundly. But as I speak my lawyers are applying for an amendment to the order."

"It's too late for that," shouted a man in the crowd. He pushed his way to the front, rain running down his glasses, striped pyjamas tucked into his green wellies and a wad of papers in his hands. ˏ

"And you are…?" asked Godric disdainfully.

"Neville Clearly," said the man. "Chief planning officer." He swept a hand along the crowd. "Like everyone here, I had a dream tonight. It was as if you were talking to me as you are now."

"You dreamed of me?" Godric smiled. "I'm very flattered."

"We all dreamed of you," shouted a lady with a pitchfork.

Godric frowned, his eyes flicking across faces as he hurtled towards a terrible realization.

"You were telling that girl there about a Roman temple buried in this wood," said Neville Clearly. "Then a huge flock of birds woke me, and that's when I noticed the voicemail left for me by an investigative reporter named Misty Meadows. She said you were moving in on the wood two days and four hours early, Mr Thorn. This, I presume, was the same Ms Meadows who delivered to me earlier this week a file showing gas deposits to be nowhere near this spot. I had dismissed that report as erroneous but now I smelled a rat."

"He smelled a rat," murmured the crowd.

"So I called the council's historic environment record officer. She too had experienced the same dream, but she was ahead of me."

As the crowd broke into applause, a short lady with round glasses stepped forward. She was wearing a dressing gown under her mackintosh.

"Carrie Smith," she announced. "Historic environment record officer. You mentioned mosaics from Ephesus and priests from Patara, Mr Thorn, so I drove to the archive to check the records, and you know what I found? Nothing."

"See?" Godric smiled again. "No rat."

"But the reason I found nothing was because the ground-penetrating radar survey carried out in 2008 had been removed from the records. Luckily there are duplicates held in Norwich, so I called my friend and, well, look." She held up her phone but no one could see it, so she explained. "Clear evidence of the extensive and carefully organized architectural remains consistent with your assertion, Mr Thorn, of the existence of a dismantled temple complex."

A gasp of surprise rippled through the crowd.

Neville Clearly stepped forward. "On that evidence, Mr Thorn, planning permission is hereby revoked subject to investigation under the Ancient Monuments and Archaeological Areas Act 1979."

Godric held up his hands and bowed his head. "That's fine, Mr Clearly," he said. "I'd rather we made extra sure there's nothing of value under that wood besides the gas." He stepped smartly onto the bulldozer and sat behind the wheel. "In the meantime, I shall take my bulldozers back to the depot and await further instructions." He revved the engine, sending out a cloud of black smoke and drowning out the cheering crowd.

Beside the bulldozer, Lee looked at Trev. Trev looked back. Lee nodded and, dragging Ace with them, the pair joined the jubilant onlookers.

Someone grabbed Orla's arm. Isaac, from the traveller site, with his sister Beatrice.

"Come with us, quick," ordered Beatrice.

"Don't argue," added Isaac.

The pair dragged her down to the riverbank. Dave covered their exit, then joined them, wagging his tail when he saw Raven.

"We need to get out of the firing line, witch girl," she said. Her right eyebrow was split, the eye was swollen shut and sticky streaks of nearly dry blood had left tracks on her face and neck.

Orla threw her arms around her. "I thought you might be dead!"

"After merely being walloped in the face by a high-pressure hose, thrown from a moving vehicle into the road and beaten by GasFrac security men until Dave saw them off? Not even close," said Raven. She nodded at Isaac and Beatrice. "These two saved me and showed me the shortcut to the wood. But we need to get out of here now." She pulled Orla towards the river. "I can't believe he fell for it."

"Fell for what?" hissed Orla.

"Confessing to the whole of Norfolk though your Traumnebel." Raven gave a lopsided grin. "He'll never live that down with the Knights of the Old Legion, so I rather suspect he's going to want you dead."

"He can't kill me," said Orla. "He made a promise that he can't break."

"What promise?"

The roar of an engine blew Orla's answer away. Screams erupted from the crowd as Godric drove the bulldozer, orange light flashing, through the fence and into Anna's Wood.

"We've got to stop him!" Orla cried.

"No, we don't," said Raven, grabbing Orla's arm. "He's already been stopped. He's just making it worse."

Orla shook herself free. "You don't get it," she said, and took off, leaping across the smashed fence with Dave at her side. Ahead, red lights came on as the bulldozer stopped at the riverside. Orla saw Godric leap from the cab, chainsaw in his hand, then watched him stride up the steep bank that hid the remains of the temple to Diana. He marched from tree to tree, jerking the starter rope on the chainsaw until it roared into life. He found the Orla Perry Tree of Life and swung the spinning chain into the trunk.

With a whoosh a cloud of magpies mobbed him, aiming for his ears, his eyes and his hands. Godric pulled the chainsaw from the tree and whirled it around his head, scattering the birds. As he turned back to the tree, the magpies attacked again, screeching in fury.

Suddenly a powerful light, brighter than the moon, punched through the canopy and Anna's Wood echoed with the clatter of helicopter blades. More lights pinned the man with the chainsaw and the wood crackled with radio chatter. Two police officers in body armour sprinted past Orla; two more appeared at the top of the mound. They had Godric Thorn surrounded but he ignored them, his face red with shiny wet magpies' kisses as he focused on cutting through the oak.

Raven arrived at Orla's side. "What's happening?" she gasped breathlessly. But with the helicopter overhead, the screeching of the furious magpies and the whine of the chainsaw it was hard to hear what the officers were saying.

Orla watched one remove a yellow taser from his vest and point it at Godric. He shouted something in vain, so he shrugged and pulled the trigger. The effect was instant as Godric dropped the chainsaw and fell into the leaves, his body shaking in uncontrollable spasms. The helicopter banked away as more police arrived, bathing the Orla Perry Tree of Life and the prone body of Godric Thorn in cold white light.

The chainsaw was switched off, and as Godric was pulled to his feet and handcuffed, Orla heard a police officer say, "Godric Thorn, I'm arresting you on suspicion of four counts of aggravated criminal damage; two counts of unlawful imprisonment of a minor; and one count of the unlawful imprisonment of a police officer. I am also arresting you on suspicion of reckless endangerment to life."

Godric gave a murderous glare as the police officer brushed a wet leaf from his expensive black coat.

"You do not have to say anything but it may harm your defence if you do not mention when questioned something which you later rely on in court. Anything you do say may be given in evidence. Do you understand, Mr Thorn?"

As the helicopter swung away, Orla ran to the oak. He'd managed to cut halfway through and might have succeeded in felling the tree had it not been for the magpies. A white feather drifted past, splashed in blood, and the lifeless body of a black and white bird lay at the base of the tree. Gently Orla picked it up, noticing that it had only one foot.

The crowd jeered as Godric was led out of the wood, his coat torn, his shiny black hair awry and his face bleeding from the kisses that would show him his future. He hissed at the villagers, then glanced back over his shoulder at Orla.

"Remember our deal, Orla Perry," he called, "and look after that tree. It probably won't last the year."

"What deal?" asked Raven as Godric was dragged away.

"A witches' deal," muttered Orla, scooping her wet, bloody and very muddy dog into her arms.

A police Land Rover stopped at the edge of the crowd and first Richard then Tom stepped out.

Richard grinned. "Sorry we're late. Did we miss anything?"

"I didn't see what happened to Tom but I saw them dragging you up the lane," said Orla, scanning her brothers for injury. "I didn't know what to do."

Richard looked at the crowd, at the broken fence, at the abandoned bulldozers and at Godric Thorn being led away in cuffs.

"Looks like you knew exactly what to do," he said. "I thought you said the Traumnebel had failed."

"Clearly not," said Raven.

"Richard got locked in Godric's weird black car," said Tom. "I tried to rescue him and got caught too. Then

299

a policeman got locked in with us and had to smash the window to get us out." Then he noticed Isaac and Beatrice. "Hello again," he smiled.

Suddenly Dave squirmed in Orla's arms and broke free. He'd just remembered he had an urgent matter to attend to. He slipped through the crowd, fast, low and unseen as he closed in on his target. Godric had just stepped into the dazzling lights of the police Land Rover and the BBC Look East crew, his head held high in defiance. The four arresting officers had no time to react as eight and a half kilos of toned terrier burst from between the onlookers' feet, launched himself like a rocket and sank his teeth deep into the prisoner's rear end. As the policemen struggled to pull the Jack Russell from Godric's left buttock, the wickedest Knight of the Old Legion let out an unholy squeal.

Dave held on as long as he could and then, as Godric's shredded trousers slipped into the mud in the glare of the TV cameras, he released his grip and disappeared.

Werewolf One reporting: mission accomplished.

The crowd went wild.

AFTERMATH

The TV crews stayed until sunrise to file live reports of the Battle of Anna's Wood for the breakfast bulletins.

"We should get out of here," said Richard, watching as cameramen and -women shot pictures of bulldozers sitting like burned-out tanks on a cold battlefield while presenters with umbrellas pestered locals for interviews.

"We should try and persuade your uncle to see a doctor," said Raven, wiping the rain from her face.

"Can someone take a picture of me on this D10T2?" called Tom, hoisting himself onto the bright yellow Caterpillar that had come so close to crushing his sister.

"Absolutely not," sighed Richard. "We were never here, right?"

He looked down at Orla's backpack and the stuffed cat sat beside it.

"What are we going to do about Vinegar Tom?" he wondered. "Should we auction him for charity?"

"Take him home with us," said Tom, jumping off the bulldozer. "He can go on my shelf."

Raven grimaced. "What a gruesome way to spend eternity." She picked up the stuffed cat, brushing the mud and the water from his coat and giving him a scratch behind a damp, moth-eaten ear. "This cat saved the day, you know. Without the sprowl he had hidden inside him, the Traumnebel would never have happened." She looked up at Richard and Tom, then down at Dave. "And that man would have killed us all."

"In really imaginative ways," added Richard.

Orla was stood apart from the others. She'd just buried the one-footed magpie at the edge of the wood and was now staring into space, listening to the birdsong and quietly counting her blessings. As long as the oak was safe, then the gang would be safe. Between them, she, Uncle Valentine and Mr Flaherty would protect the tree, and, evil as he was, Godric Thorn was also a man of his word.

"So our rigid feline friend deserves a hero's funeral," concluded Raven. "A cat's not properly dead until he's buried."

Orla wheeled on Raven. "What did you just say?"

Raven frowned. "We were talking about Vinegar Tom. I was saying a cat's not properly dead until he's buried."

Orla nodded. She held out her hands. "Give him to me."

Tucking the stuffed cat under one arm, she hoisted her backpack onto her shoulder and walked towards the wood. Dave stretched, let out a long sigh and limped after her. He was:

Never.

Off.

Duty.

His wasp was still with him. It had seen off the woodpecker and was more of a friend now than a pest.

"Where are you going?" called Richard.

Orla kept walking. The dawn chorus was deafening – the birds singing for the pure joy of living.

"A cat's never dead till he's buried, remember?" she called over her shoulder. "I reckon old Vinegar Tom has got a couple of lives left in him yet." Then she turned to face them, her red curls dripping with rain and a big smile splitting her mud-splattered face.

"And I know a spell for that."

Photograph © Ray Wells

C. J. (CHRIS) HASLAM is a multi-award-winning journalist at *The Times* and *The Sunday Times*. He appears regularly on the BBC and has written three black comedy thrillers for adults. One of them, *Twelve-Step Fandango*, was shortlisted for the Edgar Allan Poe award. *Orla and the Serpent's Curse* was Chris' first book for children. He lives in Cambridge with a Jack Russell terrier called Dave.